"What do you get out of it?" Chloe asked, refusing to accept what she was hearing. It just did not make sense.

She looked up at him, biting her lower lip in consternation, desperately trying to find a rational explanation for his demand. His blue eyes caught hers and bored down into her, chasing all rational thoughts out of her head. She sensed her body responding to him again. Her heart was racing and her skin felt hot and sensitive.

"Finally a bit of color in that face," Lorenzo said, lifting his hand to cup her blazing cheek.

Chloe gasped as his fingers made contact, releasing another torrent of desire to storm through her body.

"Sex?" Her voice was no more than a startled whisper, and her eyes were wide with shock. "You want sex?"

Lorenzo raised his brows, and his full sensual lips twitched into a smile that was mocking and knowing at the same time.

"Are you offering me sex?" he asked, sliding his fingers deep into her hair and pulling her close to his hard body.

Welcome to the April 2010 collection of fabulous Presents stories for your indulgence!

About to lose his kingdom, Xavian will bed his new queen, but could she be his undoing? Find out in the first installment of our sizzling DARK-HEARTED DESERT MEN miniseries, *Wedlocked: Banished Sheikh, Untouched Queen* by Carol Marinelli. They're devastating, dark-hearted and looking for brides!

Why not enjoy two fabulous stories in one with *Her Mediterranean Playboy* by exciting authors Melanie Milburne and Kate Hewitt. Be seduced under the Mediterranean sun, where wild playboys tame their mistresses!

Isobel has never forgotten the night Brazilian millionaire Alejandro Cabral took her innocence, but when he discovers she had his daughter, he'll stop at nothing to claim her again in *The Brazilian Millionaire's Love-Child* by author Anne Mather.

Why not unwind with a sexy story of seduction and glamour—Xavier DeVasquez will have innocent Romy slipping between his sheets one more time in Helen Bianchin's *Bride, Bought and Paid For*. Sally must become Zac's mistress on demand or risk ruin in Jacqueline Baird's *Untamed Italian, Blackmailed Innocent!* And billionaire Lorenzo Valente vows to have his wedding night in *The Blackmail Baby* by Natalie Rivers.

Look out for the next tantalizing installment of DARK-HEARTED DESERT MEN in May with Jennie Lucas's *Tamed: The Barbarian King!*

The glamour, the excitement, the intensity just keep getting better!

Natalie Rivers

THE BLACKMAIL BABY

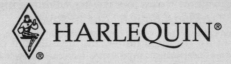

HARLEQUIN®

TORONTO • NEW YORK • LONDON
AMSTERDAM • PARIS • SYDNEY • HAMBURG
STOCKHOLM • ATHENS • TOKYO • MILAN • MADRID
PRAGUE • WARSAW • BUDAPEST • AUCKLAND

Recycling programs
for this product may
not exist in your area.

ISBN-13: 978-0-373-12912-6

THE BLACKMAIL BABY

First North American Publication 2010.

Copyright © 2009 by Natalie Rivers.

www.eHarlequin.com

Printed in U.S.A.

All about the author…
Natalie Rivers

NATALIE RIVERS grew up in the Sussex countryside. As a child she always loved to lose herself in a good book or in games that gave free rein to her imagination. She went to Sheffield University, where she met her husband in the first week of term. It was love at first sight and they have been together ever since. They moved to London after graduating, got married and had two wonderful children.

After university Natalie worked in a lab at a medical research charity and later retrained to be a primary school teacher. She began writing when her son started nursery school, giving her a couple of free mornings a week. Now she is lucky enough to be able to combine her two favorite occupations—being a full-time mom and writing passionate romances. When she has a free moment she enjoys reading, gardening and spending time with family and friends.

CHAPTER ONE

'CHLOE VALENTE, you are the most amazingly beautiful and sexy woman.'

The words were a deep, sensual purr in Chloe's ear, and a hot tingle of anticipation rippled through her body. She'd never thought of herself in that way—but as she felt Lorenzo standing close behind her, the heat of his strong body burning through her fine silk wedding gown, she knew that everything in her life had changed beyond her wildest dreams.

'Thank you for making this day so special.' She drew in a shaky breath and clung to the ornate stonework of the balcony, looking down into the fabulous ballroom, which was still buzzing with guests sipping vintage champagne. It was hard to believe that this palazzo, owned by Lorenzo's proud Venetian family for generations, was now her home. 'It's been truly wonderful. I can't imagine a more perfect wedding day.'

Venice was a magical place to be married, and a

silvery dusting of snow falling from the February sky had made it seem even more enchanting and romantic. As she'd travelled back to the *palazzo* after the ceremony, reclining on velvet cushions in a sleek black gondola beside her breathtakingly handsome groom, she'd known that this was the happiest day of her life.

'The best is yet to come,' Lorenzo promised, his Italian accent purring in her ear as he traced his fingertips lightly along her collarbone. 'Let me take you to the bedroom and show you.'

Chloe closed her eyes for a moment and leant her head back against his shoulder, letting herself drift on a wave of pure pleasure. Simply knowing how much Lorenzo wanted her sent her heart racing and made butterflies of excitement flutter deep inside her.

Then the hum of conversation mixed with the clink of crystal glasses and angelic harp music floated up from the wedding reception below.

'We can't leave now.' She pushed his hands away weakly as she felt his sensual lips nuzzling her neck beneath the sleek blonde bob of her hair. 'What about all the people?'

'You always do the right thing,' Lorenzo said, sliding his hands down to her waist and turning her to face him. 'You were the perfect PA, always anticipating my needs and those of my associates. And even now you are thinking of our guests—of being the gracious hostess.'

She gazed up into his vibrant blue eyes and a familiar frisson of elation whispered through her. Just looking at him always made her feel like that. With his smouldering good looks and superb physique he was the most gorgeous man she had ever seen. It was almost impossible to believe that he was now her husband—that she was married to Lorenzo Valente.

She'd spent two years as his PA loving him from a distance, knowing that her feelings for her incredible Venetian boss could never be reciprocated. She was an ordinary English girl, and he was from one of Venice's oldest, most noble families, in addition to being an internationally respected billionaire businessman. They'd belonged to different worlds and Chloe had known they could never be together.

But then Lorenzo had asked her out on a date.

At first it had been hard to believe. Since the day Chloe had starting working in Lorenzo's London headquarters she'd seen an endless succession of highly polished society women draped on his arm—all tall, slender beauties with smoky come-to-bed eyes and flowing manes of dark, glossy hair.

They were all the complete opposite of Chloe, who was short, blonde and curvy, with a fair, freckled complexion and pale green eyes that looked ridiculously overdone if she experimented with more than a lick of mascara and the softest smudge of eyeliner.

But despite her initial doubts—how could someone as magnificent as Lorenzo be interested in someone as unremarkable as Chloe?—he had been impossible to resist. He'd swept into Chloe's personal life like a tornado, romancing her with the fast-track intensity that typified everything the passionate Italian did.

Before long all of Chloe's reservations had been blown away. She'd seen how he'd treated his previous women as passing diversions, and she knew that he was treating her very differently.

He'd never mentioned love, but Chloe realised he wasn't comfortable with sentimental displays of emotion. He had taken her to his home in Venice and he had talked about their future—and the children he hoped they would have together. To Chloe, that was the biggest sign of love and commitment she could have seen.

She'd accepted his proposal with joy in her heart, knowing that she was entering a new, wonderful chapter of her life—a chapter that she believed would last for ever.

'Come upstairs with me, and let me anticipate *your* needs, my special little Chloe,' he said huskily. 'Let me show you how pleased I am to have married you.'

Chloe looked up into his face and felt her eyes start to grow warm with unshed tears of happiness. She had never thought of herself as special—certainly never viewed herself as sexy or beautiful. That Lorenzo had called her all those things meant more than she could say.

She gazed up at him, the love and happiness fizzing through her body more potent than the champagne she had been sipping all afternoon. And there was one wonderful thought in her head.

I love you.

Just three little words, but she'd never said them out loud. Neither of them had.

In the beginning Chloe had been too shy to admit her feelings, but now everything had changed. They were married. They'd stood up together in front of a congregation and pledged themselves to each other for the rest of their lives—and now her heart was overflowing with happiness.

Suddenly she could not help saying the words that were buzzing inside her.

'I love you.'

An immediate, terrible change came over Lorenzo—a change so profound that Chloe's words seemed to freeze and splinter in the air. Iron dread stabbed into her, and she knew that she had made a terrible mistake.

'Love?' Lorenzo's voice was hard with shock. 'Why did you say that?'

'Because…because it's true…' Chloe stammered weakly, staring at his dreadful expression.

'What game are you playing?' Lorenzo demanded, his black brows twisted incredulously. 'You know—you've always known—that's not what this is about.'

'But…' Her voice petered out and she was suddenly filled with stomach-churning anxiety. What was Lorenzo saying to her?

'You know this is a purely practical arrangement,' he bit out. 'We discussed how you would be my perfect wife. How a sensible, businesslike arrangement was far superior to an overblown emotional minefield. You always knew my feelings on the subject.'

'I don't understand.' Chloe stared at him in horrible confusion, aware that her heart had started to thump with sickening jerkiness beneath her breast.

She thought back to his proposal. It was true that he hadn't gone down on one knee to ask her to marry him, but he had taken her to Paris—the most romantic city in the world. They'd been walking along the Seine, with golden-brown autumn leaves swirling around them, when he had taken both her hands in his and asked her to be his wife.

She tried to remember his exact words—to recall how the conversation had developed. But suddenly all she was aware of was Lorenzo's angry expression as he stared down at her.

'We first discussed the matter when your mother and sister were leaving for Australia,' he said. 'I asked about your father, and whether he was emigrating with them. You told me that you hadn't seen him since your seventh birthday.'

'But you and I weren't involved back then,' Chloe said, struggling to grasp the relevance of that past conversation. 'That was before you'd even asked me out.'

She remembered how he'd been sympathetic, and how he'd made her feel better by confiding in her that his mother had walked out when he was just five years old. It was the first time their relationship had pushed the boundaries of boss and PA. He'd even poured them a drink at the bar and told her...*told her how he believed life would be much simpler without the complications of unrealistic romantic ideals.*

Chloe pressed her hand over her mouth as she remembered what he'd said. She'd never, ever guessed that he was serious—that his cynical remark was more than a passing statement driven by unhappy childhood memories.

She stared up at him in shock, trying to recall if they'd ever discussed the subject again, but she knew that they hadn't. She would have remembered if he'd said anything to make her think his interest in her was driven by cold, practical matters.

He swore bitterly and raked rigid fingers through his short black hair. Two slashes of colour now burned on his high cheekbones and his blue eyes glittered with mounting fury.

'I thought you were different from the rest,' he said. 'Not another of those women trying to trap me into marriage with false declarations of love, and promises you had no intention of keeping. But now I see you are just like all the rest—worse even, because you've waited until now, our wedding day, to do this.'

His words sank into the turmoil of Chloe's mind and she struggled to make sense of what she was hearing. She realised she was shaking and folded her arms across her body, hugging herself tightly.

'It sounds as if you are saying you don't want to be loved.' Chloe could hear the confusion and doubt in her own voice, but she pressed on, determined to comprehend what Lorenzo was telling her. 'But I don't understand. It's natural to hope for love—and to look for it.'

'People who look for love are fools,' Lorenzo said with contempt, a vein pulsing on his temple.

'But what if you find love—even if you aren't looking for it?' Chloe asked. She'd never expected to fall in love with her boss, but his magnetic charisma and dynamic assurance had made it impossible for her not to.

'Love is an illusion—a false ideal that never holds true,' he grated, staring down at her through narrowed eyes.

'You are so harsh—so cynical,' Chloe gasped. 'Of course love exists—you can't deny what your heart feels.'

'And is your heart still telling you that you love

me?' Lorenzo said derisively. 'Even now that we have revisited my feelings on the subject?'

'It's not something you can switch on or off,' Chloe said, dismayed by his attitude. She'd known he could be arrogant and overbearing at times, but she'd never thought of him as a cruel man.

It seemed there was a lot she didn't know about the man she had just married. Had she just made the worst mistake of her life?

'So you are sticking to your story?' Lorenzo asked. 'Perhaps for the sake of consistency you think it best to maintain the pretence for now?'

'What do *you* want from marriage—from your wife?' Chloe demanded, refusing to let him bully her into saying something to humiliate herself.

'I wanted someone honest and natural,' he said. 'Someone I could respect. Not another of those women whose grandiose pronouncements of love are as false as their manicured appearance.'

'I *have* been honest with you,' Chloe said, blinking furiously as she felt her eyes start to burn with tears. There was no way she was going to let herself cry in front of him, not after the way he was treating her. 'And if you can't respect that—can't respect *me*—then that's your problem.'

She lifted her chin defiantly, pressing her teeth into her lower lip to stop it quivering, and tried to push past him. But his fingers closed on her arm, biting into the flesh like a steel vice.

'Go and compose yourself,' he said, witheringly. 'But don't take too long. After all, you were the one anxious not to be rude to our wedding guests.'

Chloe drew in a startled breath, looking over her shoulder, down into the ballroom below. She had all but forgotten where she was and it was a shock to see the party still in full swing.

A wave of nausea washed through her as she wondered if anyone had seen her awful exchange with Lorenzo. But no one was looking up at them and a quick glance around assured her that they were alone on the balcony.

'There were no witnesses—which is fortunate for you—' his words were disdainful, but that did not mask the undercurrent of menace in his tone '—because I will not tolerate any further disrespect from you. Or permit you to shame me in any way.'

Chloe stared at him, suddenly unable to recognise the man she had fallen so deeply in love with. She opened her mouth to respond—to tell him that *she* wouldn't tolerate any more of *his* vile behaviour. But before she had the chance to speak he turned sharply and strode away towards his study.

She stood stock-still, watching him go—aware of the crackling emotion storming through his tall, powerful body as his long, thrusting strides bore him swiftly along the corridor. She'd never been able to look away if Lorenzo was in the room. His presence drew her gaze like a magnet.

Even now, after everything that had just happened, she couldn't look away until he was out of sight. But, as his study door closed, she knew what she must do. She had to get herself away from him—as fast and as far as possible.

Ten minutes later Chloe hesitated by the door of her bedroom, looking down at the beautiful silk wedding gown lying on the bed. She'd felt like a princess wearing that dress. Or maybe like Cinderella going to the ball. But she'd found out in the most brutal way that Lorenzo was not Prince Charming.

She shuddered, remembering his expression when she'd declared her love for him, and pressed her hands over her face, trying to blot out the memory of the caustic look in his eyes as he'd ground her hopes and dreams into dust. He'd broken her heart and callously humiliated her in one fell swoop.

For the first time she was grateful that none of her family had made it to the wedding. Her mother and sister were too involved in their new life in Australia, and since Chloe had decided not to go with them it was almost as if they'd forgotten she existed. And of course her father was not there. She didn't even know where he was—or if he was still alive.

She drew in a deep breath and forced herself into action. She'd thought that this was the happiest day of her life, but Lorenzo had woken her up from that fairy tale with a merciless jolt. Now she'd have to hurry if she wanted to have any chance of making a clean getaway. And at that moment all she wanted was to be as far away from Lorenzo as possible.

She pulled her faux fur hat tight onto her head to completely cover her light blonde hair and obscure her face as much as she could. Then she turned up the collar of her long coat and slipped out into the corridor, heading towards the side staircase that led to the *palazzo*'s water gate.

She knew there'd be many boats at the Grand Canal entrance, waiting to ferry the wedding guests back to their hotels after the reception, and she needed transportation to get across the lagoon to the airport as quickly as possible. There wasn't much time before the last plane left the city that night.

Disguised in bulky winter layers, she didn't look anything like the petite blonde bride who had arrived that day, radiant with happiness and fresh from her wedding ceremony—and she desperately hoped that no one would recognise her. She couldn't bear it if one of Lorenzo's security staff dragged her back inside—back to Lorenzo.

She shivered as she climbed into a water taxi and gave directions for Marco Polo Airport. An icy wind that felt as if it had blown straight from the frozen spires of the Dolomites sliced right through her and started her shivering deep inside.

That afternoon the sparkling flurries of snow had seemed beautiful and romantic. Now the weather seemed unrelenting and cruel.

But at least she'd got away from the *palazzo* unchallenged, and was on her way across the dark lagoon to the airport. The windows of the boat were completely misted over so that she couldn't see anything, and the movement of the water was making her feel sick.

Suddenly the night seemed impenetrable—a swirling black and white uncertainty, with no visible landmarks. And her heart was breaking into a million tiny fragments that were no different from the icy shards of snow blowing down from the mountain peaks, to be swallowed up by the ink-black water of the lagoon.

Lorenzo stood outside on the balcony, staring into the snowstorm in a temper that was as foul as the night. The snow was falling so thickly that the lights shining from the buildings on the other side of the Grand Canal were just a dim glow, and there was no way to see any distance across the open water.

Not that there was anything to see. Chloe was gone.

She had boarded the final commercial plane to leave the city that night, and now the weather made it impossible for him to follow—even in his private jet.

He swore bitterly, gripping the balustrade with

fingers that were as cold and hard as the stone beneath them.

He knew where she was almost certainly heading—to the home of her best friend, Liz, in a small village south of London. But as a precaution he had people waiting at Gatwick Airport to track her onward journey and to confirm her final destination.

It was not a long flight. In fact she was probably nearly there by now. He lifted his arm automatically to check his wristwatch, and cursed again as he saw that the face of his watch and his dark wedding suit were covered with icy white snow.

He turned abruptly and stepped into the bedroom, dashing the snow away with rough, impatient sweeps of his hands. But it was already melting with the heat of his body, so he shrugged his wet jacket off and tossed it aside.

Suddenly he froze—staring down at the wedding dress Chloe had abandoned on the bed. His heart thudded violently in his chest and he felt his blood surge angrily through his veins.

How dared she walk out on him like this?

How dared she turn tail and run away into the night?

The end of their marriage was not *her* decision to make on a whim, simply because he had quashed her sentimental outburst.

But that was immaterial now. He did not know

or care whether her declaration of love had been a calculated ploy. Or if it had been a simple misguided notion brought about by the grandeur of the occasion. It made no difference now. By running away she had sealed her fate. Their marriage was over.

He picked up the dress and found himself picturing how sexy Chloe had looked wearing it. He'd spent most of the afternoon imagining peeling it slowly off her delectable body.

He had truly believed that she would be a good wife. That she would make a good mother for his heirs.

But their union had been short-lived—finished before it had even begun.

A sudden, unwelcome memory flashed through his mind, and he clenched his fists, unaware that he was crushing the delicate fabric in his hands. This was not the first time someone had walked away from him at the *palazzo*. But no one would ever get away with it again.

He looked down at the soft silk dress. Then, with an abrupt, violent movement, he threw it savagely out onto the balcony.

He stood, staring at it for a moment, forcing himself to breathe slowly and consciously bringing his pounding heartbeat back under his control. In the eerie light of the storm the dress already looked indistinguishable from the snow that had settled on the stone balcony. If the weather didn't let up, it would soon be covered.

He slammed the glass door shut. Then he turned his back and walked away.

CHAPTER TWO

Three months later.

IT WAS a beautiful day in early May. The sun was shining, the birds were singing. And Chloe stood at the graveside of her best friend, holding an orphaned baby in her arms.

It was almost impossible to believe—but it was true. Liz, baby Emma's mother, had really gone. Chloe had had three months to come to terms with the fact that her dear friend was losing her battle against cancer, but somehow her death had still come as a shock.

She'd flown from Venice on that bitter night in February and travelled straight to Liz's country village home. She'd been desperate to see her friend—partly to talk about what had happened with Lorenzo. But mostly just to seek the comfort of her company.

But when Liz had opened the door of her cottage

and beckoned her inside, Chloe had known at once that something was wrong. The cancer that they'd hoped and prayed would stay in remission had come back.

Liz had delayed telling Chloe because she didn't want to spoil what was supposed to be the happiest day of her life—her wedding day. And even more heartbreaking was the news that the disease had progressed too far for the doctors to save her.

Chloe looked down at the baby snuggled in her arms, feeling cold and empty. The May sunshine did nothing to take the chill away, and at that moment she felt as though she'd never be warm again.

'Are you all right, love?'

She recognised the concerned voice of Gladys, Liz's kindly neighbour. The old lady had been an incredible support during the past weeks. She'd helped to keep up her spirit at the bleakest of times, and offered to look after the baby, enabling Chloe to spend as much time as possible with Liz at the hospital, and then later on at the hospice.

Chloe turned and tried to make her smile convincing, although she knew Gladys was unlikely to be fooled.

'I'm fine,' she said.

'It was a lovely service,' Gladys said. 'The readings Liz asked for were beautiful.'

Chloe nodded, swallowing against the hard lump of sorrow that was constricting her throat. She had found the funeral almost unbearable. The pain of losing her best friend was still too raw. Liz had been too young to die. And baby Emma was too young to lose her mother.

'If you're sure you're all right, I'd better get back to the cottage,' Gladys said gently. 'They'll all be waiting for me by now.'

'Thank you for inviting everyone back for tea,' Chloe said gratefully. It had been thoughtful of the old lady to offer to host a small gathering after the funeral, and something Chloe just didn't feel up to.

'It's the least I could do.' Gladys brushed her thanks aside. 'You've got your hands full with little Emma. And you've already done so much.'

'I only did what anyone would have done,' Chloe said.

'No, not anyone,' Gladys said stoutly. 'You took good care of your friend during a difficult time. And now you are doing a wonderful thing—taking on her baby as your own. Liz was truly blessed to have a friend like you.'

Chloe pressed her trembling lips together and tried to smile at her. She knew Gladys meant well, but at that moment it was hard to think of Liz as blessed. She'd suffered so much, only to have her life snatched away by cancer.

'I'll see you in a little while.' Chloe gave Gladys a hug. Then, as the old lady turned to head back towards the row of terraced cottages in the village, she quietly breathed a sigh of relief. She needed to be alone for a moment.

She couldn't face being squeezed into Gladys's tiny front room with the crowd of well-meaning mourners from the village. Liz had not had any close relatives and Emma's father had never been part of the picture. From the moment he'd discovered Liz was pregnant he'd wanted nothing whatsoever to do with her, and even claimed that there was no way he could be the father.

'We'll be all right,' Chloe whispered, and kissed Emma's soft cheek. 'We've got each other.'

But as she pressed her face against Emma's wispy baby hair, she suddenly felt very alone.

She found herself thinking about Lorenzo. Three months ago she'd thought she was about to embark on the most wonderful journey of her life— marriage and children with her gorgeous Italian husband. Now everything was so different.

She had not heard a word from him since the night she left Venice, and that had hurt her more than she wanted to admit, even to herself. She'd known it was unrealistic to hope that he would follow her, saying that he'd got it wrong, and that he did love her after all.

But still, that was what she'd wished for.

She had not contacted him either. She'd been too involved with caring for Liz and Emma. And, if she was completely honest, she hadn't been able to face him.

Deep down she knew she'd behaved badly by running away without talking to him—but she'd simply reacted instinctively to the discovery that Lorenzo viewed their marriage as a loveless practicality. An overpowering need for self-preservation had kicked in, and she'd known that to protect her broken heart she had to get away from him.

But now she *had* to contact Lorenzo.

Firstly about her intention to adopt Emma. They were still officially married, and that might cause complications with the legal procedures. And secondly, about some money she'd been forced to use a couple of days earlier, from an account he'd set up in both their names before the wedding. The amount she'd taken would be nothing to a man as rich as Lorenzo, but she knew him well enough to be aware that no detail—no matter how small—ever escaped his notice.

She wanted him to know that she would pay him back as soon as she could. She had no wish to take anything from him. And the sooner she set things straight, the sooner she could put that heartbreaking episode of her life behind her, and get on with building a life for herself and Emma.

A tremble ran through her at the thought of seeing Lorenzo again, but she closed her eyes and pressed her cheek against the top of Emma's head.

'I'm not going to think about that now,' she said

to the baby. She'd promised Liz that she'd think happy thoughts, but at that moment it was a hard promise to keep.

She walked across to a wooden bench under a flowering cherry tree. The soft grass was scattered with the delicate pink blossom and it reminded Chloe of confetti.

Suddenly tears welled up in her eyes. It was the most beautiful day. But her best friend was not there to share it with her. And she never would be again.

Lorenzo Valente handled the convertible with a natural ease, shifting gears smoothly as he approached a tight bend in the winding country lane. It was a fine afternoon in May and the sun felt surprisingly warm on his shoulders as he sped along the leafy green road in rural England.

He usually enjoyed driving, but the expression on his face was far from one of pleasure—he was thinking about the latest stunt Chloe had pulled.

Very little shocked Lorenzo. He accepted the fact that being born into a wealthy family, and then multiplying that fortune by several orders of magnitude, had made him a target for various types of gold-digging parasites.

However, he'd never thought *Chloe* would steal from him. But it was just one more thing to make her pay for.

His strong fingers tightened on the steering wheel

and his eyes narrowed dangerously. A minute later he reached a tiny village. He slowed the car, and took the turning that led to the church. He drove a short distance along the narrow lane and then pulled up onto the grass verge, waiting for the crowd of pedestrians leaving the church to pass.

He knew that it was the day of her friend's funeral. He'd seen to it that he had been kept very well-informed about Chloe's actions since she walked out on him.

Suddenly he caught sight of a small figure dressed in dark grey walking unsteadily across the churchyard.

It was Chloe.

A strange sensation lodged in the pit of his stomach and he felt his heart start to beat faster. He was out of the car in an instant, ignoring the curious looks he was drawing from some of the villagers. He only had eyes for Chloe.

He strode across the churchyard towards her, the soft grass muffling his footsteps. She did not see or hear him approach, and sat completely motionless on the bench beneath the flowering cherry tree, engulfed in a private moment of sorrow.

He was about to speak but he hesitated, feeling an unaccustomed stab of uncertainty. Her eyes were closed as she wept, tears sliding silently down her white cheeks as she held a baby nestled in her arms. Her grief for her friend was so personal—he knew that his presence was an intrusion.

Suddenly she opened her eyes and stared up at him. A flash of surprise passed across her features.

'Lorenzo.' Her wide green eyes were luminous with tears in the warm afternoon sunshine, and her pale skin looked almost translucent. 'Oh, God, I can't believe you're here.'

Hearing her say his name with such feeling sent an unexpected surge of emotion powering through his veins. He wanted to reach out and smooth the moisture from her cheeks, but instead he clamped his arms stiffly by his sides.

'Really?' he said, knowing his tone was harsh, especially after witnessing the depth of her grief. But the intensity of his reaction to her had caught him off guard. He wasn't accustomed to being affected by other people's emotional displays. 'I thought that, by stealing my money, it was your intention to draw me out.'

'The money…that's why you're here?'

Chloe looked up at him, her pulse still racing from the shock of opening her eyes and seeing Lorenzo standing there. He looked so strong and vibrant—and, despite everything, he was the most welcome sight in the world.

For a moment she let herself believe that maybe he was there because he knew she needed him—knew how sad and alone she felt. She had no doubt that he was aware of everything that had happened to her since she'd left Venice. Information was another essential currency to Lorenzo.

'What other reason could there be?' he said, his piercing blue eyes boring into her.

She drew in a breath, suppressing the irrational surge of disappointment that rose up within her. But really she'd known that, if Lorenzo cared for her at all, he would have come before this.

'I'm going to pay the money back,' she said. 'I needed it urgently.'

'For what?' Lorenzo demanded. 'What was so urgent that you couldn't wait until you found some other way of paying? That you needed to take my money immediately and without permission?'

'I had to pay for this,' Chloe said, sweeping her arm around with a distracted gesture, unable to believe how cold and unfeeling he seemed. 'My savings are gone, my credit card is maxed out. I've had no income for months, but I've been looking after Liz and…'

She stopped abruptly, suddenly wishing she hadn't said so much. The state of her finances was none of Lorenzo's business.

It was a shock to find herself face to face with him again, and one heartbreaking thought kept going round in her head: he had no interest in *her*—only in what he thought she'd taken from him. Could he really have come all this way to berate her over the comparatively small amount of money she'd spent?

'I used the money to pay for the funeral,' she stated bluntly. Surely even Lorenzo wasn't so hard-hearted that he would begrudge that.

'You should have asked me,' he said coldly.

'I didn't need to ask,' she said. 'The account is in both our names. I never wanted to use a penny of that money, but I'm not going to apologise for it, because I'd do it again in a heartbeat. Liz deserved a proper funeral.'

Lorenzo stared down at Chloe, registering an undercurrent of uncertainty showing through her expression despite her continued defence of her actions. He knew she was still emotional, and he felt unwelcome feelings churn in his own stomach in response.

This was not what he had expected when he'd married Chloe—that three months after their wedding they would be meeting for the first time in an English churchyard and arguing over a stranger's funeral expenses.

He'd chosen her to be his wife because he thought she'd be reliable and stable, the way she'd been as his PA. He wanted his marriage to be straightforward and uncomplicated, not like the often hysterical and unpleasant scenarios he'd wit-nessed growing up as his father worked his way through a string of unsuitable wives.

But nothing had worked out the way he intended. Chloe had walked out on him. Then she'd chosen not to get in touch—even when she was in financial trouble.

'You were too proud to ask for help,' Lorenzo said. 'You'd sooner steal my money than talk to me.'

Chloe let out her breath with a resigned sigh and looked straight up into his eyes.

'I didn't think you'd let me use the money. I thought you'd freeze the account or something,' Chloe said. 'You didn't really know Liz. You only met her a couple of times.'

Lorenzo swore with sudden violence. Then frowned at the baby as she started to grizzle and fuss in Chloe's arms.

'What kind of man do you think I am?' he demanded angrily. 'You truly think I'm so petty I would not pay for a funeral?'

Chloe stared up at him with wide eyes that seemed huge in her pale face, looking as startled as the baby by his loud outburst.

'I don't know,' she said, her voice sounding shaky and uncertain. 'We might be married but it seems I don't know you at all.'

Then she looked away, down at the baby in her arms.

'I can't do this now.' She rocked Emma gently and murmured soothing words to her. 'She's probably hungry. It's been a long afternoon and I need to get her back to the cottage.'

She looked small and awkward standing there, wearing an ill-fitting charcoal-grey suit that swamped her tiny frame and was pulled out of line by the baby in her arms. The unforgiving colour drained any speck of warmth from her fair complexion and her light blonde hair hung down in a shapeless curtain nearly to her shoulders.

Next to the fresh green grass and colourful pink blossom she looked starkly monochrome, almost as if she'd stepped out of a black-and-white movie—some old-fashioned, overblown melodrama.

She didn't belong here—not like this.

The anger that had gripped Lorenzo suddenly dissipated. He had to get her away from this place. It was impossible to talk to her in the churchyard.

'We'll go together—just to pick up what you need,' he said. 'Then you're coming with me.'

Chloe stared up at him in surprise. She hadn't expected him to start issuing orders—although that was exactly how Lorenzo was used to behaving with most people in his life. And it was how he had been with her too, back before they became personally involved.

'I know you're angry with me,' she said, 'but you can't just sweep in here and boss me about. I don't work for you any more.'

'No. You're my wife,' Lorenzo grated, the tone of his voice telling her that he was far from happy about that. 'And you are coming with me.'

'But I have Emma now,' she protested, tightening her hold on the infant protectively.

'What about her father?' Lorenzo asked, studying the crying baby with a crease between his brows.

'He never wanted anything to do with her,' Chloe said. 'I'm the only one she has now.'

Lorenzo lifted his eyes to Chloe's face, and an expression she couldn't read passed across his features.

'Let's go.' He reached out and took her arm before she realised what he intended.

As his hand made contact it was as if a jolt of energy surged through Chloe. She gasped and looked down automatically, staring as his strong fingers closed around her upper arm, tanned and vital next to the dull grey fabric of her jacket.

Her heart started to beat faster, and at that moment she felt the numbness that had deadened her over recent days start to thaw.

Lorenzo was only holding her arm, but suddenly she was fully aware of him physically—aware of his sheer size and strength. And shockingly aware of the body heat radiating from his powerful, athletic form.

She found herself drawn towards him, like a flower turning towards the sun.

She'd been so cold and lonely. All at once she found herself longing to feel his strong arms around her—to press herself against the solid masculine expanse of his chest.

Suddenly she realised that Lorenzo had stopped moving. He was standing utterly still. And she knew, even without looking up at him, that he was taking in her reaction to his touch.

A flash of alarm shot through her. She couldn't let Lorenzo see how vulnerable she was feeling, how in need of physical comfort. He'd always been able to read her like a book, and right at that moment her defences were lower than normal.

'I'm not going anywhere with you,' Chloe said, trying to shrug out of his grip. But his fingers simply tightened, and with Emma in her arms it was impossible to struggle too much.

'There are matters we must discuss,' Lorenzo said, turning her round so once again they were facing each other.

Chloe shook her head, staring directly ahead—straight at his broad chest. She did not want to talk to him any more. And she definitely did not want to look into his perceptive eyes.

She had the terrible feeling she would reveal herself to him in some way—let him see how naked her emotions were, how much she craved his presence. The day had already been too painful. The thought of him driving away and leaving her alone again suddenly seemed unbearable—but there was no way she would admit that to him.

'Your desertion on our wedding day made it clear that you are no longer happy with our arrangement,' he said, cupping his free hand under her chin and lifting her face to his.

Her gaze was locked to his clear blue eyes again and the touch of his fingers against her skin made her shiver once more.

'I didn't think we had an *arrangement*,' she replied, feeling a chill creep back around her heart. His words were a harsh reminder that she had been disastrously wrong about what their marriage meant to Lorenzo—about what *she'd* meant to him.

'Yes, we did,' Lorenzo said, 'which is why we need to talk. There will be no further misunderstandings between us.'

CHAPTER THREE

CHLOE sat in the limousine with Lorenzo and Emma as it purred along the narrow lanes away from the village where she'd lived for the last three months. It was late in the afternoon but the sun was still shining brightly. Billowing drifts of frothy white cow parsley lined the roadside, and the hedgerows were a mass of lacy hawthorn blossom.

Chloe stared out at the passing countryside, hoping to calm her jangling nerves. She could not let herself look across at Lorenzo. She was still too unsettled and confused by her feelings towards him.

She'd spent the last few weeks desperately missing him, despite the fact that she knew she was yearning for something that did not really exist. Everything she'd believed to be true about their relationship had been false. Lorenzo did not love her. All he'd wanted was a convenient wife.

But now he had appeared out of the blue, and her body and soul had responded to him with an intensity that had knocked her off balance. It was as if her mind had no influence over what she was feeling towards him—or even as if the heartbreaking revelation on their wedding day had never really happened.

'I gather that your friend had no immediate family.' The sound of Lorenzo's deep voice startled her. She turned to him, feeling her pulse crank up a notch once more the moment she met his steely blue gaze. 'But where are the rest of her relatives?'

'There aren't any,' she said, dragging her eyes away from his face with surprising difficulty to look down at Emma, who was asleep in the infant car seat beside her. 'That will make the adoption more straightforward. It's what Liz wanted—and what I want too.'

'Adoption is a serious commitment. And a legally binding arrangement,' Lorenzo said. 'Did you not think it would be appropriate to discuss your intention with your husband?'

His voice was level and the tone neutral, but Chloe knew it was a pointed comment. She turned back to him and saw that he was staring at Emma. There was a deep crease between his black eyebrows and Chloe realised she'd never seen him in such close proximity to a baby before.

He was looking at Emma as if she were a tiny alien who had somehow sneaked into his car.

She knew that Lorenzo wanted children—they'd

discussed it after he asked her to marry him. At the time she assumed he'd be a wonderful father. But now, judging by his expression as he studied Emma, she wasn't so sure. Perhaps he just wanted children to inherit his legacy and carry on his family name.

Chloe had always wanted to be a mother and now she had a baby to care for. It wasn't the way she would have wanted it to happen, but when she promised Liz that she would adopt Emma she'd known that the baby girl was the most precious parting gift her friend could have given her.

'There's no need for you to worry,' she said, feeling instinctively protective towards Emma. 'The adoption will not affect you.'

As soon as she'd spoken she felt his temper flare once more and a prickle passed across her skin. The limousine suddenly seemed too small, and she wished they were back in the open air again.

'We are married,' he grated. 'I imagine that the adoption courts will be interested in that—even if you think you can act as if we are not.'

'I'm not acting as if I'm not married!' she snapped, meeting his gaze straight on. 'I'm just trying to do the right thing for an orphaned baby. My promise to adopt Emma has nothing to do with you.'

His piercing gaze held hers and the air between them seemed to vibrate with sudden tension.

Chloe swallowed reflexively as she realised how angry he was that she'd made this decision without him. He was probably thinking about how the adoption would affect him legally, and whether he would have unwanted responsibilities towards somebody else's child.

'You won't stop me doing this,' she said. 'Nothing will stop me taking care of Emma. No one will ever take this baby away from me.'

But at that moment she realised that Lorenzo *was* involved. Until they were divorced, he might have some influence over the adoption procedure.

'I *will* fight for Emma,' she added, still staring straight into his hard eyes. Her heart was beating quickly and she felt the muscles of her face grow taut as she continued to maintain eye contact. But she wouldn't look away. She couldn't cave in so easily. There was too much at stake.

'We're here.'

Lorenzo's voice broke the silence and Chloe let out a shuddering sigh, turning away to see where he'd brought them. He'd told her he had somewhere private near by where they would be able to talk, and she hadn't asked any more questions.

The idea of somewhere different, away from the cottage that held such sadness, had been very appealing. She'd quickly packed a few things, telling herself that he was right—they did still have issues that needed to be resolved. But deep down she'd known that she didn't really want to be alone at the cottage that night.

'Where are we?' she asked as they drove through an impressive brick arch. Wrought-iron gates swung silently closed behind them, then she caught her first glimpse of a sleek modern house, set in the most beautiful grounds. 'What is this place?'

If this was where Lorenzo was staying, no wonder it hadn't taken long for the limousine to come out to the village, bringing an additional driver to return with Lorenzo's convertible.

'It was your wedding present,' Lorenzo said shortly as the limo purred along the sweeping drive-way up to the front door. 'You left before I had a chance to give it to you.'

Chloe blinked in surprise, totally lost for words. She knew she ought to say something, but her mind had gone completely blank.

She realised Lorenzo was already out of the car, waiting for her to join him, so she leant across to release the safety belt that held the infant car seat securely in place. Then before she had a chance to move Lorenzo reached in and lifted the portable seat, complete with sleeping baby, out of the car.

Chloe followed him into the house with a very strange feeling running through her as she watched him carrying Emma. It was clear that he was taking care, but even so it looked more as if he were carrying a basket of groceries at the supermarket than a little baby. All of a sudden that thought struck her as absurdly funny—she just couldn't imagine

Lorenzo Valente carrying a basket of food around a shop—and she bit her lip to stop herself smiling.

But then as quickly as the flash of humour had struck her, it vanished again. And she found herself trailing behind him through a beautiful house into an incredible glass-walled living room, which overlooked a stunning landscaped garden.

Lorenzo placed Emma's carrier carefully onto a cream rug and turned to speak to her.

'Chloe, this is Mrs Gill Guest, the housekeeper,' he said, gesturing a middle-aged lady forward from a doorway at the side of the room. 'Mrs Guest, I would appreciate it if you would assist my wife. Help her and the infant to settle in, and discuss any particular requirements she may have, especially regarding the baby.'

Then, without another glance in her direction, Lorenzo turned on his heel and strode out of the room, his leather-soled shoes making no sound on the natural wood floor.

Lorenzo marched through the house to his study, tension screaming in every muscle of his body. He shut the door behind him, flung off his jacket and tugged at his tie, suddenly feeling unbearably constrained.

Just a couple of hours in Chloe's company and already he was reaching the edge of his control.

He had come to England to bring his marriage to Chloe to a decisive end—but not until he'd sought retribution for what she'd done. She would not get away with walking out on him.

In theory it should be easy to take the situation back into his own hands. He'd seen how Chloe responded to him when he touched her, and he knew that she was desperate for him to give her the comfort she'd needed.

That was exactly what he intended to do. Then afterwards, once he had made her realise what she had walked away from, what could have been hers for life, he would ruthlessly sever the relationship.

His plan was perfect with its elegant simplicity.

But he had wanted her with a fierceness that had taken him by surprise—a need so overpowering that it had threatened his rational command.

Even now the fire was burning in him, making his throbbing body ache for her relentlessly, despite the fact she was now out of his sight. Three months was a long time and, although he'd considered their marriage over in all but name, he had not taken another woman to his bed.

No one had caught his eye—not one woman had stirred the same magnitude of desire within him.

When he'd looked down at her standing beside him in the churchyard, the urge to drag her against him and crush her soft pink lips with his mouth had been almost irresistible. Passion had pulsed through his veins like molten lava, until the only thing he could think about was making love to Chloe.

He could not let it go on. He would not let his physical desire cloud his mind any longer. Chloe had already caused enough disruption in his life. He would take her to bed and get her out of his system. Once and for all.

But, deep in the dark recesses of his mind, he knew once would not be enough.

Chloe stood in the bedroom, by the floor-to-ceiling plate-glass window, staring out at the stunning view across the rolling green hills. It was a beautiful place, and exactly the type of house she'd once dreamed of living in. It reminded her of a property she'd visited and fallen in love with as a child, and she was certain that Lorenzo must remember her telling him about it.

The building was modern, with clean, simple lines and wonderful airy living spaces with masses of huge windows that made it feel continuous with the garden and the lush green countryside that surrounded the house.

It was an incredible wedding gift. Not because of its value, but because it had been chosen personally for her, in answer to a childhood dream that she'd never expected to have fulfilled.

But now she was there she almost wished Lorenzo had taken her to an impersonal country hotel, because she didn't know how to interpret his purchase of this house. It was so close to Liz's village that it could not be a coincidence. And, if he had given it to her before the wedding, she would have seen him buying a place near her best friend's home as a sign of his love. Now she was just horribly confused.

She lifted her chin and shook her hair back from her face—pushing those thoughts firmly from her mind. All she should be thinking about was how to secure her future as Emma's adoptive mother. From Lorenzo's reaction it was clear he was angry that she hadn't kept him informed about her intention. She knew that she would have to tread carefully, because she could not—*would not*—let anything stop her adopting Emma.

A gentle tap on the door pulled her out of her thoughts, and she realised it was Mrs Guest return-ing to babysit while she went down to talk to Lorenzo in his study. A knot of anxiety tightened in her stomach, but she did her best to ignore it and smiled at the older lady.

'Thank you for staying with Emma.' Chloe glanced over at the baby sleeping in the cot that Mrs Guest's husband had set up earlier that evening. 'She doesn't normally wake once she's down for the night, but it's such a big house I was worried I wouldn't hear her if she does.'

'It's my pleasure,' Mrs Guest said. 'The baby-monitoring equipment will be delivered tomorrow, but I'll always be happy to sit with her.'

'Thank you,' Chloe said, wondering how long Mrs Guest expected her to be staying there at that house—whether Lorenzo had given his staff any indication. 'You've been very kind.'

She left the bedroom and walked slowly down to Lorenzo's study, butterflies crashing in her stomach and her heart beating apprehensively.

In the past she'd always looked forward to seeing him. During the two years that she'd been his PA she'd eagerly awaited business arrangements that would bring him to his London offices. Then, once their relationship had moved on to a personal level, she'd spent every minute they were apart daydreaming about when they would be together again.

But now she knew he was angry with her. And the enforced wait to see him had made her nervous. She smoothed her hands down over her clothes, wishing that she hadn't changed into her jeans and a T-shirt. But the grey suit had been borrowed from Liz's wardrobe, and it had been too upsetting to wear it any longer.

She walked down the curved staircase with her gaze fixed on the open door of his study, realising that he would be able to see her coming. She started to tread as quietly as possible, thankful that her flat ballerina pumps made virtually no sound.

Suddenly Lorenzo appeared in the doorway. His blue eyes locked on to Chloe instantly, sending a rush of nerves skittering through her, which was quickly followed by a heated jolt of sensual awareness.

He looked absolutely magnificent—the epitome of masculine good looks and animal magnetism. Tall and powerfully built, his broad-shouldered athletic form would make heads turn wherever he went. But it was so much more than his physical presence that made an impact—the sheer force of his personality emanated from him, despite the fact he was standing absolutely still, wearing an unreadable expression.

Chloe took a steadying breath and forced herself to keep walking down the stairs.

'Come into my study,' Lorenzo said, standing aside just enough to let her brush past him. 'We still have a lot to discuss.'

It was another impressive glass-walled room with sliding doors that opened directly onto a wide decking area next to a large fishpond edged with a mass of flowering purple irises.

But Chloe was only conscious of Lorenzo as she slipped through the narrow gap he'd left for her, feeling the heat of his body even in the brief moment it took to slip past. She felt tiny next to him, especially in her flat shoes. For an instant she wished again she hadn't changed out of the formal grey suit—but then she pushed the thought aside.

She might be small, but she was a strong woman.

She would not let herself be overwhelmed by Lorenzo. She'd been through such a lot over the last three months, and this conversation with Lorenzo was just another hurdle to get over. She might as well get on with it—on her own terms.

'I'm sorry that I didn't tell you about my intention to adopt Emma,' she said immediately, seizing the opportunity to speak first. 'I understand why you are upset about it, but it doesn't have to have any impact on you at all.'

'Of course it does,' Lorenzo said. 'Don't be so foolish—we're married.'

He stared down at her impatiently. His body was already responding to her presence—she looked as sexy as hell in her figure-hugging jeans and T-shirt. But for the first time he was struck that he hardly recognised her as the woman he'd married just three months earlier. She seemed so different.

It was clear that she hadn't had much time to spend on her appearance, but that was understandable. She looked tired and washed-out, and her freckles were more pronounced than ever against her milky complexion.

Her pale blonde hair had grown out of the sleek, tailored bob into a shapeless, uneven curtain that brushed her shoulders, with a tendency to fall forward and obscure half of her face. Her clothes were verging on scruffy and her flat shoes had seen better days.

The physical differences were distracting, but what he really found disconcerting was the change in her attitude. She had behaved badly and, even though she'd just offered him a partial apology, there was still a determined set to her shoulders and a defiant thrust to her chin.

'No, it needn't affect you—not if we hurry the divorce through before I take the adoption any further,' Chloe said.

A flash of anger surged through Lorenzo and for a moment he could not believe what he was hearing. Chloe had walked out on him on their wedding day without a backwards glance, and now she had the audacity to tell him this!

It was unacceptable—there was no way that he would tolerate Chloe telling him their marriage was over.

'No.' The word fired out of him like a bullet. 'There will be no divorce.'

'Why not?' Chloe gasped, staring at his furious face in disbelief. 'After all the things that have happened, I thought it was what you would want.'

'It is *not* what I want,' Lorenzo grated. 'A string of broken marriages is exactly what I intend to avoid.'

'One divorce is not a string of broken marriages,' Chloe said. 'Anyway, this is hardly a marriage. It was only a few hours after the ceremony when I found out that you didn't…' She hesitated, searching for words that were not too painful to say. The memory of him saying that he didn't want her love had haunted her every day for the last three months. 'I had to leave. We could probably even get an annulment if you don't want a divorce.'

As soon as she had spoken, she knew it was a mistake. A storm of powerful emotions raged across Lorenzo's face but before she had a chance to react he stepped forward and seized her upper arms, pulling her roughly towards him.

'We may not have made love on our wedding day,' he grated, lifting her onto her tiptoes and leaning down so their faces were only inches apart, 'but that doesn't mean that this union was never consummated.'

Sexual energy crackled in the air between them, making it hard to think straight. But Chloe knew that was all it was. Just sex.

'We never made *love*!' She struggled in his vice-like grip, trying to pull away—but her mind was spinning with images of the many mind-blowing nights she'd spent in his arms. 'That was the problem. I thought it meant something—that what we had was real. But it was all meaningless. You misled me into this marriage. Surely that alone is enough to make it null and void!'

'It was never meaningless,' Lorenzo said.

He glowered down at her, his expressive black eyebrows drawn low and menacing, and there was a dangerous predatory glint in his eyes. For a moment Chloe half expected him to kiss her—and to her utter confusion and shame she almost wanted him to.

'Well, it clearly didn't mean the same to you as it did to me,' she cried as she finally managed to wrench herself out of his hold.

She stood her ground and met his eyes boldly, aware that she was still easily within the reach of his strong arms. That knowledge sent a startling jolt of excitement through her, and she felt her cheeks start to burn. She lifted her chin and glared up at him, desperately trying to ignore the way her pulse rate was suddenly responding to his physical proximity.

Her body might be attuned to his—every inch of her skin tingling with a growing desire to feel his hands on her again. But it was just hormones. Emotionally he was a million miles away.

'You have no idea what our marriage meant to me,' Lorenzo said.

'No, I don't,' she agreed, remembering the confusing and heartbreaking argument they'd had on their wedding day, 'but I do know that *I* thought I'd found my soulmate—my partner for life. Instead, all I'd found was a lie!'

'I never lied to you,' Lorenzo said, 'and I thought the same thing as you—that I had found *my* partner for life.'

'How can you say that?' Chloe demanded. 'After everything you told me about not believing in love, how can you say that?'

'Because that is what I wanted,' Lorenzo said, 'and it is what you agreed to when you married me.'

'But…'

It was impossible to think with his penetrating gaze holding her captive. She sensed her body responding to him again. Her heart was racing and her skin felt hot and sensitive. She tipped her head a little further back and frowned, trying to make her gaze cold and stern—but the feel of her own hair brushing her shoulders felt like a caress, sending a ripple of sensual anticipation through her.

'Finally, a bit of colour in that face,' Lorenzo said, lifting his hand to cup her blazing cheek.

Chloe gasped as his fingers made contact, releasing another torrent of desire storming through her body.

'Don't touch me,' she said, in feeble protest.

'Why not? You want me to,' he said. 'And you still owe me our wedding night.'

'Our wedding night? You mean sex?' Her voice was no more than a startled whisper and her eyes were wide. 'After everything that has happened—everything we've said—you want sex?'

Lorenzo raised his brows and his full, sensual lips twitched into a smile that was mocking and knowing at the same time.

'Are you offering me sex?' he asked, sliding his fingers deep into her hair and pulling her close to his hard body.

CHAPTER FOUR

'YOU know I'm not offering you sex!' Chloe exclaimed. She tried to step back, out of his grip, but he held her firmly.

'That's what it sounded like,' Lorenzo drawled, leaning down and brushing his lips across the sensitive skin he had exposed by lifting her hair up off her neck.

A delicious shiver skittered down her spine, and he was holding her so close that she couldn't help letting him feel her very physical response to his gentle kisses. Trying to hold her body stiff and straight in denial of how she was feeling was pointless—he knew her well enough to know that she was suddenly yearning for him to make love to her.

But it was *not* love, she reminded herself. That made a difference. That *had* to make a difference.

But then why was her body slowly melting into his embrace? Why was she becoming pliable in his arms, as he arched her backwards and brought his mouth down on hers?

He kissed her with devouring heat, ignoring her feeble attempts to pull away, as he plundered her tender mouth in an overwhelmingly sexual on-slaught. His body was big and strong, but it wasn't his sheer physical size and strength that overpow-ered her. It was the fervour of her own response to him that left her defenceless.

Her eyelids slid down and she was lost in a moment where only she and Lorenzo existed. She was aware of his potent virility with every inch of her body. His tongue moved against hers, making her want more—so much more that she trembled with pure, naked desire. Her blood was singing in her ears and her whole being was buzzing with longing.

His hands skimmed over her, then suddenly he swept her right off her feet and up into his arms.

Her eyes flew open in surprise, and her conscious mind plummeted mercilessly back to the cold light of day. Her body was still yearning for Lorenzo, muddling her grip on the situation, but she knew she had to stop him before things went any further.

Intimacy was not love. Chloe knew that she was fooling herself if she let herself believe a true con-nection could form between them, when Lorenzo felt no love for her.

'Put me down,' she gasped, pushing her hand

against the powerful wall of his broad chest and staring up into his face.

He stood still, as solid as a rock, and held her gaze with his own. She knew what he must see in her eyes—after all, she could see the same thing glowing in his: smouldering arousal.

'On the desk—or the sofa?' he asked, his voice dangerously deep and loaded with sexual intent.

Chloe swallowed reflexively, trying to stop her mind replaying the many times they'd made love on his desk. And on various bits of furniture, and in other unusual places. During the time they'd been lovers they'd often been so wrapped up in their passion for each other that they failed to make it to the comfort of their bedroom.

At the time she'd found it thrilling. And she'd taken it as proof of the depth of his feeling for her. Now the knowledge that Lorenzo wouldn't hesitate to get physical in almost any location filled her with a mixture of excitement and panic.

'Three months is a long time,' Lorenzo said, lifting her slightly so that his face was only inches above hers. 'I've waited long enough.'

'You waited…' Chloe drew in a shaky breath and stared at him, lost for words.

Somehow, over the months they'd spent apart, it had never occurred to her to think of Lorenzo with another woman. Now that suddenly seemed naive. She knew what a hot-blooded alpha male he was, and she knew he had never spent long without a woman in his bed.

'Did you think I'd taken another lover?' he asked, his voice harsh with an emotion she couldn't identify.

'No, I…' She hesitated. 'I never thought about it until now.'

A sudden flare of anger crossed his face as he dumped her back onto her feet.

'You never thought about it!' Lorenzo exploded. 'You didn't care enough about the man you professed to love to wonder whether he'd replaced you in his bed?'

She stared up at him, suddenly feeling cold away from the warmth of his arms, despite the huge and intimidating way he loomed over her. But she realised her words had been an affront to his masculine pride.

'It wasn't like that,' Chloe said. 'You know what the last few months have been like for me.'

'No,' Lorenzo barked. 'I don't know. You walked out of my life—the life I thought we were building together—and shut me out completely.'

'What did you think I would do when you denounced my love?' Chloe cried, spiralling back to the soul-crushing moment in the *palazzo* on their wedding day. 'I opened my heart up to you—and you were angry with me! You tore my heart to pieces and shredded everything I believed in.'

'I did not expect you to turn your back on me—on our marriage—so easily,' Lorenzo replied. 'You said you loved me. Then you behaved as if I was nothing to you.'

'What was I to you?' Chloe demanded. 'Someone you tricked into marriage for your own convenience—someone you didn't care enough about to be honest with?'

'You were my wife.'

Lorenzo's voice was hard with the clipped tones of finality. He turned abruptly and strode towards the door of the study.

Chloe stared after him, feeling as if a hurricane had just ripped through the room. Her heart was racing and her scalp was prickling with the static electricity—but now that neither of them was speaking the space was filled with an unnatural silence.

Suddenly, just as his hand reached the door handle, Lorenzo turned and fixed her with his penetrating eyes.

'You are still my wife,' he said. 'And that is how it will stay.'

He closed the door behind him and Chloe sagged against the desk, feeling all the strength drain out of her body.

She'd felt as if a hurricane had torn through her, but she knew the quiet emptiness was simply the eye of the storm. It wasn't over yet. In fact it was going to get a whole lot worse before she was out the other side.

Chloe climbed back up the stairs to the bedroom where Mrs Guest was watching over Emma. Her eyes felt warm with the telltale heat of tears, but she blinked them back, refusing to let them fall. She didn't have the resilience to cope with the kindly housekeeper's sympathy. She knew her heartache was something she would have to deal with on her own.

'There you are, dear,' Mrs Guest said, smiling warmly as she walked back into the room. 'The little darling hasn't stirred since you've been gone.'

'Thank you,' Chloe said, returning the older woman's smile.

She crossed the room to look down at Emma, who was lying in exactly the same position as when she'd left her. It seemed like hours since she'd gone down to see Lorenzo, but in fact she realised only very few minutes had passed.

'You look wiped out, dear,' Mrs Guest said. 'Why don't I stay a few more minutes while you relax in the bath? You don't want to be popping your head in and out of the en suite all the time, wondering if the baby is still sleeping.'

'Thank you.' Chloe accepted the offer gratefully, suddenly desperate to lock herself safely away from the world—or, if she was completely honest with herself, away from Lorenzo. She had no idea where he was and it was perfectly possible that he could appear at any moment. She knew that he had been using this bedroom too, and right at that moment she couldn't bear the thought of coming face to face with him again. 'But actually I'll take a shower,' she added, trying to keep her voice from cracking with the wave of emotion that was rising up through her. 'I think I'm too tired for a bath.'

She locked the bathroom door and a sob broke raggedly from within her. She clamped her hand over her mouth so that Mrs Guest wouldn't hear and stumbled across the room, shedding her clothes as she went.

A moment later she turned on the shower. A torrent of warm water gushed out and she stood beneath it, finally letting go of the tears that she'd been holding back for so long. She wept with abandon, unable to control the anguished sobs that racked her slender body.

Eventually, all cried out, she leant back against the tiled wall and smoothed her hands over her hot face. Everything had come together in an unbearable build-up of misery. And at that moment it was impossible to separate her grief for her friend from her distress over the intolerable situation she'd found herself in with Lorenzo.

The water continued to pour down and she

reached automatically for the shampoo. For a few minutes she would take refuge in everyday necessities and routines.

A little while later, wrapped securely in a fluffy white bathrobe, Chloe emerged from the en suite. Mrs Guest put down her book and looked up with a smile.

'Mr Valente popped in,' she said, making a knot tighten inside Chloe's stomach. 'He said that unfortunately he had to work late. But because he knew how tired you were, he would sleep in the guest room tonight—he said he didn't want to disturb you or little Emma.'

'Thank you for telling me,' Chloe said. As Mrs Guest left, closing the door behind her, she wondered what the older lady had made of the message. While she and Lorenzo had been together they'd never slept in separate bedrooms.

Chloe crawled into bed and tried to sleep, but although she was exhausted she couldn't relax. All she could think about was Lorenzo's final comment that she would remain his wife.

She couldn't understand why he had said that. It didn't seem to make any sense. Deep in her heart she longed to stay married to Lorenzo—she still wanted everything she had wanted when she accepted his proposal to be his wife.

But the situation was completely different

now. She had Emma to consider. And now she knew that he did not love her.

The following morning Chloe found herself alone in the house. Or rather, Lorenzo was not there. Mrs Guest was in the kitchen and her husband was working in the garden.

Chloe busied herself looking after Emma, but her mind was full of confusing thoughts about the future, making it impossible for her to relax. So she carried Emma out into the garden, hoping to find a way to distract them both.

Once again she was struck by what a beautiful place Lorenzo had bought. Chloe knew he hadn't intended it to be their main home—he would never leave the grand Venetian *palazzo,* which had been in his family for generations. But this house with its clean modern lines and light, airy feel made a very pleasant complement to the ornate, history-filled palace.

'Good morning!' Mr Guest appeared around the corner of the house carrying a box, which appeared to contain some kind of baby's toy.

'Hello.' Chloe smiled. It was a relief that Lorenzo had employed such a friendly, down-to-earth couple to look after the house. She'd always felt slightly uncomfortable around his formal and super-efficient staff in Venice.

'I thought the little one might like a turn in this.'

He held up the box and Chloe realised that it contained a high-backed baby's swing seat. 'I don't know how old she is, but it says on the box that it's suitable for infants six months and up.'

'She's five and a half months now,' Chloe said, looking down at the baby in her arms, 'but she holds herself well, and I'm sure she'd love to try it.'

She followed Mr Guest back round the corner, to a charming children's play area, complete with swings, slides, a climbing frame and a covered box that Chloe assumed was a sandpit.

'This is amazing,' she said as she watched Mr Guest attach the swing seat to the wooden frame. 'Did the previous people have children?'

'I don't think so. Mr Valente had this done when he bought the place. I know neither of you realised you'd have a little one so soon, but your husband is obviously very keen on kids. There we are,' he added, stepping back and eyeing his work to ensure the seat was hanging level. 'Give that a try.'

'Thank you,' Chloe said, as she carefully secured Emma in the seat and gave her a little push. But Mr Guest's comment about Lorenzo had taken her aback. She'd never thought of him as being keen on children. And after she'd seen him with Emma the previous day, the opposite seemed more likely to be true.

'She likes that!' Mr Guest chuckled as the baby gave a squeal of delight. 'I'll leave you to it, then.

If you need anything, just give me a shout. Or call my wife—that's the back door to the kitchen right there.' He picked up the empty cardboard box and his tool bag, and headed off around the house.

Chloe glanced up and saw Mrs Guest through the kitchen window. She lifted her hand to wave, then turned back to Emma, who was clearly having a wonderful time in the swing.

But Chloe's thoughts were on Lorenzo, and his attitude towards children.

As far as she could remember, she'd never actually seen him interact with any babies or older children—although that hadn't ever seemed unusual because no one they spent time with had a young family.

But yesterday in the limousine he'd seemed truly uncomfortable around Emma, and that had made Chloe start to wonder if he only wanted children inherit his Venetian legacy. Now she realised that *must* be the reason why he'd married—to secure himself an heir.

She pushed her hair out of her eyes, unaware of the cloudy expression on her face.

'Hello, Chloe.'

Lorenzo's deep voice startled her, and she spun round to see him standing just a few feet away. He was dressed in a dark suit, as if he'd just come from a business meeting, and his clothing seemed incongruous in the garden, especially standing next to a wooden climbing frame.

'Why did you marry me?' she suddenly blurted. 'If love didn't come into it—then why did you pick me? I'm short and ordinary-looking. I have no money or connections. You could have had anyone you wanted. Why me?'

'I already told you,' Lorenzo said, without missing a beat. 'Because I thought you'd make a good wife.'

'Don't you mean a good *mother*?' Chloe accused him, tipping her head back to shake the hair out of her eyes. 'You just married me to have children.'

'You want children too,' Lorenzo replied flatly but, despite his level tone, his gaze slid across to the baby in the swing seat. 'In the circumstances, it's fortunate that you didn't marry someone dead set against children.'

'You heartless beast!' Chloe exclaimed, snatching Emma up into her arms.

'No, I didn't mean—'

'Save your smooth-talking explanations,' Chloe cried. She held Emma high against her shoulder and she bent her head over, pressing her cheek against the baby's soft, wispy hair. 'You say you want children and that I'll be a good mother—but what about you? What kind of father will you be? All you've done is stare at Emma like she's some kind of impostor!'

She glared up at him angrily, suddenly hating how cool and controlled he looked. For the last three months her life had been horribly out of her control—it wasn't fair that he could stand there looking so calm.

'You have to give me time,' Lorenzo said. 'I have nothing against the infant, but she has arrived rather abruptly in my life.'

'She doesn't have to be in *your* life—I keep telling you that!' Chloe exclaimed, scraping her hair back from her face with a desperate gesture. 'How can you be so heartless? Her mother died!' she cried. 'My best friend died, and all you care about is my wish to adopt her baby.'

Suddenly her eyes were swimming with tears and a second later she was weeping.

Lorenzo stepped towards her immediately. Then he wrapped his arms around her sobbing body and gently drew her close. She leant into him instinctively, clinging to him, and finding solace in the familiar strength of his embrace.

She hardly noticed when Mrs Guest lifted Emma carefully out of her arms. A corner of her mind knew that the baby was safe and she closed her eyes, shutting out everything but the solid comfort of Lorenzo's body. Despite everything, he was her anchor—strong and warm, and exactly what she needed to combat the cold emptiness inside her.

* * *

A little while later, when the storm of tears had passed, Chloe opened her eyes and realised that she was cradled against Lorenzo's chest. He was holding her snugly and she was still clinging to him, her hands tangled tightly in his shirt, deep inside his open jacket. They were sitting on a bench looking away from the house, across an impressive view over the meadows.

For a moment she lay completely still, amazed at how comfortable she felt in Lorenzo's arms. But then a subtle change came over him—a slight shift in his muscles and a stiffening of his posture—and she knew that he was aware that she had roused.

She sat up slowly, suddenly feeling awkward. She had no idea how long she had wept or how long she had clung on to him. It was embarrassing to have let go of her emotions so completely in front of him.

'Emma?' she asked, her voice hoarse from crying.

'Mrs Guest has her,' Lorenzo said, realigning his jacket as she pulled away from him and sitting up straighter. 'She's fine. But how about you—do you need anything? Some water, maybe?'

Chloe nodded, suddenly realising she was really thirsty, and almost immediately Lorenzo passed her a small bottle of water. It was beaded with condensation and still cold from the fridge, and Chloe took it gratefully.

Presumably Mrs Guest had brought it out for her. It was wonderful to have someone look after her for a change. And it was even more wonderful to sit with Lorenzo, knowing that he'd been there to comfort her.

'I'm sorry,' Chloe said. 'Sorry for causing a scene like that.'

'You have nothing to apologise for,' Lorenzo said. 'Your grief is entirely natural and I don't want you to think you have to suppress it because you are here with me. I can't imagine how hard the last months have been for you.'

Chloe felt her heart turn over at his sympathetic words. She knew he was sincere, and it touched her deeply.

She turned sideways on the bench and looked at him. His arms around her had felt so natural, and now his clear blue gaze appeared completely open and understanding.

It suddenly seemed vital that they were honest with each other. After the mistrust and discord between them, she longed to find a genuine connection with him. And, as she remembered his impassioned outburst the previous evening, she realised that her actions since their marriage had left him out in the cold.

On the day of their wedding she'd been brokenhearted, and at the time she'd felt that her desperation to get away from him was justifiable. It had been devastating to be told by her new husband that he did not believe in love. But she hadn't waited for the situation to calm down. She had not given him a chance to explain.

'You upset me badly on our wedding day, but I'm sorry for how I behaved,' she found herself saying. 'For running away without telling you I was going. And for not getting in touch about Emma.'

'That's behind us now,' Lorenzo said.

His tone was clipped, and with a flash of irritation Chloe knew he was never going to admit that her behaviour had had any emotional impact on him. She'd been willing to take a step towards him—but he was not prepared to meet her in the middle.

'But we still have the future to think about,' Chloe said. 'You said last night that you want us to remain married. But, given everything you have said to me—that you don't love me, that you don't even believe in love—I don't know how I can do that.'

She paused, and looked at him utterly seriously. He appeared calm, but she could see a vein pulsing on his temple, and she knew that she was on dangerous ground. But she had to get things straightened out. Her future—and Emma's future—depended on it.

'I'm not even sure if you meant it,' she said carefully. 'Or if you were just saying it because you were angry with me again.'

Lorenzo stared at her, a spike of annoyance stabbing into his gut and a band of tension tightening across his shoulders.

Chloe was right. The previous evening he *had*

reacted instinctively—striking back at her presumption that she could be the one to call an end to their marriage. But since then he had taken time to reevaluate the situation.

He had originally wanted a wife to provide him with an heir, but he had no faith in marriages based on sentiment and emotion. He wanted a stable, non-materialistic woman, who would stand by the commitment of marriage and motherhood, and not abandon her children as soon as the going got tough. Or, even more reprehensibly, sell out if she got a better offer.

Chloe had seemed to be a good candidate—until she ran out on him on their wedding day. But now things were different. She had Emma. And she had demonstrated a tenacity—a commitment to motherhood—that had made him reconsider.

'I meant it,' Lorenzo said, looking straight into her cloudy green eyes so that she would know he was sincere. 'I expect us to remain married.'

'I can't do that,' Chloe said. 'I can't stay in a loveless marriage, and I won't bring Emma up in an environment like that.'

'How will you care for her?' Lorenzo asked. 'Yesterday you pointed out that you have no job. Your savings are gone and your credit card is at its limit.'

'I'll manage,' Chloe said hotly, flashing an annoyed look in his direction. She'd known the day before that it was a mistake to let him know about her precarious financial situation—and here he was, less than twenty-four hours later, throwing it in her face.

'How?' Lorenzo pressed. 'It doesn't sound like an ideal starting point.'

'It's really none of your business,' Chloe said, but suddenly she knew that he wouldn't care about that. As far as he was concerned he had a right to know everything—and he would keep digging until he found out. 'The rent on Liz's cottage is paid till the end of next month, and I'll get a job at a temping agency in a nearby town,' she said. 'Gladys, Liz's neighbour, will watch Emma till I can afford proper childcare. It won't be long until I'm up on my feet again.'

'It hardly sounds ideal,' Lorenzo said. 'Wouldn't you rather Emma grew up as part of a family, with you to look after her, and other children to play with?'

'Other children?' Chloe repeated, appalled by his assumption and the added barb of emotional blackmail. 'I haven't agreed to stay in this marriage, and already you have me producing children like a brood mare. Is that all I ever was to you? A convenient baby-making machine?'

'A *baby-making machine* is not a mother,' Lorenzo said harshly. 'I chose you because I knew you would be an excellent mother. You care deeply about family and about commitment. You have values that are important to me, which I consider paramount in the mother of my children. And the fact that you are willing to fight so hard for your friend's baby proves that fact.'

'How can you talk about values, when you don't even believe in love?' Chloe gasped. 'Do you expect me to give up *my* values? Give up on my right to be loved?'

'Are you going to give up on your chance for a family—on Emma's future happiness and security—to chase an illusion that doesn't exist?' he demanded.

'It does exist!' Chloe exclaimed, springing to her feet and glaring down at him.

'Really? I've never seen proof,' he said, standing up so that once again he towered over her. 'You said you loved me—then just minutes later you ran out on me. Somehow giving up on our marriage so easily doesn't seem like an expression of love.'

She stared up at him, suddenly realising that she didn't have the heart to continue arguing. She'd tried to offer him an olive branch, but all he could do was throw her love for him back in her face.

'I want a genuine commitment from you,' he said, already pushing her into a decision she wasn't ready to make. 'An absolute assurance to pledge yourself to this marriage and the family we will have together.'

Chloe blinked in surprise, almost unable to believe what she was hearing. But deep down she knew Lorenzo was serious—that he was making her a genuine proposition. It fitted completely with everything he had ever said since their terrible argument at the *palazzo* when the truth about his feelings had come out.

There was so much to think about. In her heart she longed to remain Lorenzo's wife—but at what cost? And at what cost to Emma and their future children? Both she and Lorenzo had grown up in broken homes and she knew first-hand how devastating that could be. But would a loveless marriage be better than that—even if the parents stayed together?

Chloe did not know the answer. And she would not give in to emotional blackmail. She couldn't let Lorenzo strong-arm her into a decision that would affect the rest of her life.

'I need your answer,' he pressed, looming over her.

'Well, you can't have it,' she replied, with a voice that sounded calmer than she felt. Then she turned and headed back to the house.

Lorenzo thrust his hands into his pockets and watched Chloe walking away, feeling the muscles across his shoulders pull even tighter.

He wanted Chloe to remain his wife. Just how much he wanted it shocked him.

CHAPTER FIVE

'TAKE as much time as you need,' Mrs Guest said as she ushered Chloe out into the garden. 'It's a lovely afternoon and a bit of fresh air might make you feel more like yourself. Emma will be fine with me—she's a pleasure to look after.'

'Thank you.' Chloe smiled reassuringly at the housekeeper. She knew that she'd worried the older lady by getting so upset earlier in the day. 'I really am feeling better now. I just need a little bit of time alone, and I'd like to have a look around the garden. It truly is lovely.'

'I'll be here if you need anything,' Mrs Guest said.

The sunshine was warm as Chloe walked away from the house across the main lawn. She'd taken another shower, but when she came to get dressed again she just hadn't had the energy to be creative, so she'd simply slipped her old jeans back on with a fresh T-shirt.

Her main reason for accepting Mrs Guest's kind offer to watch Emma was that she desperately needed time alone to think. Lorenzo had given her an ultimatum: she must decide whether to stay married to him and make a true commitment to their future together—or leave him, and be left all alone with Emma.

He had been right when he'd said that Chloe was not in an ideal situation to bring up a baby on her own, but that didn't mean she couldn't do it. At least she had the type of office skills that were always in demand—and as long as she could earn sufficient money to pay the rent by the end of the month, she would have somewhere to live.

Millions of women brought up children in far less favourable circumstances—with no proper training to get a job and with no one to help out in emergencies. Gladys had been a wonderful neighbour to Liz, and Chloe knew she could count on her if she had no choice.

But should she be so quick to abandon her marriage to Lorenzo?

The flash of joy that had lightened her soul when he appeared at the churchyard the previous day had told her that her feelings still ran deep. And being held in his arms earlier had felt so right.

Now that her emotions were no longer running wild, and she had taken a moment to calm down, she knew for certain that she still loved him. Love wasn't something she could just switch on or off. It was an unfathomable, undeniable truth that filled her body and soul.

Before Liz died, Chloe had made her a promise—that she wouldn't hide herself away from life and lock up her heart because she had been hurt. But she didn't know how that promise fitted into the future Lorenzo was offering.

Should she turn her back on him and give up on the one thing she had truly wanted—marriage and a family with the man she loved? Or should she accept his offer of a secure and privileged life for herself and their children—and give up on her heart's deepest wish to experience a genuine loving relationship?

It was an impossible choice.

Lorenzo stood by the glass wall of his study and watched Chloe walking along the far edge of the pond, beside a drift of purple irises. Her head was bowed and, although her blonde hair had fallen forward to obscure her face, he knew she was deep in thought. After all, he had given her a lot to think about.

She looked tiny in her jeans and T-shirt, but Lorenzo was getting used to seeing her that way, which was nothing like the way she'd dressed when they were together. When she was his PA she had always dressed smartly for work, and, although her style had been less formal once they were personally involved, she'd always looked well-groomed.

Now the difference in her appearance seemed to underline the difference in their relationship. She looked small and fragile as she sat down on a bench, and as she lifted her head to shake her hair back from her face Lorenzo could see that she was frowning.

Her gaze drifted across the pond, then settled on the huge windows of Lorenzo's study. She was looking right at him, although he knew she couldn't see him because the glass had been treated to protect the privacy of his study. He stared back at her, feeling an unexpected jolt of irritation.

Life had been so good, with all his plans for the future falling into place nicely. Why had she gone and complicated everything? He lifted his hand abruptly and, without fully registering his intention, he hit the control that opened the large sliding doors.

Chloe was lost in her thoughts as she gazed across the pond. The sudden movement as the glass door slid silently open brought her back to her surroundings with a start. Then the sight of Lorenzo stepping purposefully onto the deck made her catch her breath in surprise.

She stared at him in shock, slowly realising that she'd foolishly sat down in view of his study. She wasn't ready to talk to him yet. She was nowhere near ready to decide what to do about his proposition.

He moved swiftly along the deck, then without breaking his stride he turned onto the gravel path that tracked the edge of the pond. He was bearing down on her so quickly that she felt her heart start to race.

She sprang up, ready to face him, although she was filled with the overwhelming urge to bolt. How had things got so difficult between them that the sight of him approaching made her want to run and hide?

She squared her shoulders and stood as tall as she could. She was *not* afraid of Lorenzo. And she would not shy away from the situation he had put her in.

'If you've come to pressure me for an answer, you're wasting your time,' she said. Her voice was clear and steady, and did not reveal how uncertain she was feeling. 'I have not reached a decision yet.'

Lorenzo came to a halt a few feet away from her—close enough for her to be reminded once again of his sheer size compared to her. But not so close that she had to crane her neck back to meet his eyes. He had discarded his jacket but he was still wearing the same white shirt as that morning.

Her eyes settled on the clusters of creases where she had balled her hands in the fabric of his shirt while she wept, and a disconcertingly vivid memory of lying with her face against his chest flashed through her mind.

'You are struggling to decide what is best for

your future,' Lorenzo said, 'and I want you to understand why I believe this is the best arrangement—for everyone.'

'You already told me your reasons,' she said quietly. 'Now it's up to me to think this through. It's an important decision I need to work out for myself—decide for myself.'

'I understand that,' Lorenzo said, 'but committing to this marriage, and to raising a family with me, is a huge undertaking. I want you to make this choice with your head, not with your heart.'

Chloe frowned, trying to make sense of what Lorenzo was saying.

'But marriage is something you feel in your heart,' she said, unsettled by Lorenzo's sudden change of tack. Why was he trying to *persuade* her into this, rather than continue trying to tell her what was the right thing to do? 'When you proposed to me in Paris, I was so happy. And I truly believed you felt the same way I did.'

'I *was* happy,' Lorenzo replied. 'I thought that I had found the perfect woman to share my life with—the perfect, uncomplicated partnership based on friendship and compatibility. Not on an over-hyped emotional ideal that would inevitably disintegrate over time.'

'Not all marriages fail,' Chloe said, suddenly feeling defensive and sad at the same time. 'You shouldn't be so pessimistic—it's depressing.'

'Not pessimistic—*realistic,*' Lorenzo said. 'In my experience most marriages do fall apart, and it usually gets pretty ugly. Then the children are the ones who suffer the most.'

Lorenzo looked down at her, reading the emotion written in her expression. She was normally such a positive-thinking, forward-looking person—which was one of the attributes that had drawn him to her in the first place. It was disturbing to see her look unhappy.

'It doesn't have to be that way,' she said. 'Happy marriages and functional families do exist.'

'Neither of us experienced it as a child,' Lorenzo said, 'but that is why this arrangement can work for us. I know you want Emma, and your own children when we have them, to grow up in a stable environment.'

'I know that *I* would never abandon my children,' Chloe said. She looked up at him, the silvery green surface of the pond reflected in her eyes, 'but how do I know I can trust you?'

Lorenzo met her gaze, already knowing how intensely she was committed to motherhood. He knew how far she would go for Emma. And he knew she'd fight equally hard for her own children.

Lorenzo's mother had not bothered to fight for him. In fact she'd used him as a bargaining chip in a massive divorce settlement. What kind of mother would do something like that?

Suddenly he found his thoughts hurtling back to his childhood—to a time that he'd thought that he had blotted out of his memory. And all at once he was remembering the hurt, disappointment and confusion as acutely as the day his mother walked out.

He shook his head sharply, and focused on Chloe again. Her face was pale and worried, and he knew what she was thinking.

'I get it,' he said, his eyes boring down into hers. 'You're scared I'm going to leave you. It's happened to you before—first your father, then your mother and sister. Even…' He hesitated, reluctant to upset her more, but he had to make his point. 'Even your best friend left you.'

Chloe swallowed, the lump in her throat making it painful, and blinked back tears. How did he know her so well—yet so little at the same time?

'I'm not going to leave you,' Lorenzo said. 'That's the beauty of this arrangement.'

'But…what about when someone else catches your eye?' Chloe asked. A dark shadow moved across Lorenzo's face and she knew she had offended him with her comment, but she had to carry on—her future was at stake. 'You don't love me—what happens when you meet someone you do love?'

'Be careful what you say,' Lorenzo said through gritted teeth. 'Don't forget what happened. You are the one who left—the one who abandoned this relationship.'

'It wasn't like that,' she protested.

'Even though you *thought* you loved me,' Lorenzo said, 'even then—with your own fear of abandonment so strong—*you* left. Not me.'

'That was different,' Chloe said. 'I'd just found out you didn't love me.'

'Do you still love me?' Lorenzo asked.

'I… No…' Chloe faltered, dropping her gaze and staring at the wide expanse of his chest. She couldn't meet his eye, or surely he would know the truth. She did still love him, but she couldn't expose her heart to him any more. It was just too painful.

'My point exactly,' Lorenzo said, his voice dripping with irony. 'You *thought* you loved me— but you were fooling yourself, living in a silly romantic dream world. It wasn't real, which is why you were able to walk out on me without a second glance.'

His fingers slipped beneath her chin and he lifted her face to look into her eyes. Chloe met his blue gaze and a frisson ran through her. The emotion she saw in the depths of his eyes was intense.

He said he didn't believe in love, but she could feel how deeply he was committed to the future he was proposing. He wanted a stable, contented family as much as she did.

'We were good together,' he said, letting his hand slip back so that he was cradling her head. 'This could be incredible. *We* could be incredible together.'

'I don't know…' Chloe started to speak, but the feel of his hand was distracting.

All she knew was she wanted to be with him. She wanted things back the way they had once been, when he made her feel special and safe at the same time.

'Make this decision with your head, not your heart,' he repeated. 'Tell me that you want to stay married to me. That you want to raise a family with me. That you want to be my wife in every way.'

'Yes,' she said. 'Yes, I do.'

But she was speaking from her heart. It was impossible to do anything else. Her heart was calling out so loudly to him that she could not have heard anything her head was saying even if she'd tried.

'You've made the right choice,' Lorenzo said, pulling her towards him.

Chloe closed her eyes as he enfolded her in his arms. It felt so good, as if she truly belonged there.

Then his hands started to move across her body, and she knew that he intended to make love to her. A quiver of apprehension mixed with anticipation tingled through her. She had just agreed to this—to be his wife in every way.

But she was suddenly nervous, as if this exact moment was the moment of no return in her life.

From this point on her future was mapped out, and before she knew it she would be a mother. She would be bound in marriage to a man who didn't love her—a man who did not even believe in love.

'What is it?' he asked, pulling back and holding her where he could meet her eyes. 'What's wrong?'

'It's too soon,' she said, tightening her fists to emphasise her words and realising to her shock that once again they were tangled in his shirt, gripping the fabric tightly. 'I'm not ready.'

'Not ready?' Lorenzo repeated. He slid his hands across her back in a way that sent shivers through her whole body. 'You know that won't be a problem for long.'

'No—I need more time to get used to this,' she said, unfurling her hands from his shirt and taking a step backwards. But his long arms were still around her, preventing her from moving very far away. 'Let me go. Let me go so I can think.'

Almost to her surprise, Lorenzo dropped his arms to his sides and stepped away, his feet crunching on the gravel path.

He stood completely still, looking down at her from beneath heavy lids. She knew how much he wanted her, and that thought sent a rush of desire storming through her.

Making love had always brought them closer, made the connection between them stronger. Surely it would do the same thing now. She had to give their new understanding a chance, but she wasn't ready to completely sign away her future.

'I'm not ready for more children,' she said. 'Everything has been so unsettled…there's Emma to consider…it's just too soon to rush into something so big.'

'I agree,' Lorenzo said, reaching into his pocket and pulling out a little foil-wrapped package. 'Making babies can wait. This, however, cannot,' he finished huskily, hauling her towards him and covering her mouth with his.

CHAPTER SIX

THE burning heat of arousal erupted through Lorenzo's body, and he dragged Chloe closer still, lifting her onto her tiptoes and bending her back to kiss her. The taste of her mouth was intoxicating, and the feel of her slender body in his arms threatened to send him over the edge.

He was holding her so close that he could feel every tremble and quake that shook her. He could tell how much she wanted him and that knowledge was setting his own senses on fire.

It was too long since he'd made love to Chloe. Too long since he'd held her naked body in his arms and brought her pleasure in every way he knew, before eventually giving in to his own explosive climax.

Now he was consumed by a sexual need so strong that he suddenly realised that he had to find somewhere private. In the past he would not have hesitated to take her right there on the bench beside the water, but he knew that this time one quick release of passion would not be enough. It would take much longer to slake the barrage of desire that stormed his body and he intended to take every ounce of satisfaction that he could.

He pulled back from his kiss and swept her up in his arms. He would take her to the pool house—they would be undisturbed there for as long as it took.

Chloe lay breathlessly in his arms, gazing up at his gorgeous face. He'd literally swept her off her feet and her heart was racing with anticipation of what was to come. Just knowing that he was carrying her away to make love to her sent a thrill of excitement skittering through her.

She had no idea where he was taking her, and she didn't care. She was only aware of the rhythmic movements of his body vibrating through her as he strode along the path away from the house. He carried her effortlessly, as if she were as light as a feather, and she revelled in his strength, remembering that he had the power to send her to unimaginable heights of ecstasy.

She hardly noticed when they reached their destination. It was only when the door clicked shut behind them that she dragged her eyes from Lorenzo's face and looked around her.

'A swimming pool,' she murmured, not really meaning to say the words out loud.

'Later.' Lorenzo's voice was thick with arousal. 'We'll swim later—now I need you naked.'

Sudden heat flared between Chloe's legs and her whole body started to quiver. She was burning up inside and she needed Lorenzo as much as he needed her.

'Put me down,' she said, wriggling in his arms. She was too restricted in his grip—she wanted to touch him, to move against him, to rip his clothes off him.

'Wait,' he commanded, striding past the pool to a lounge area beside a bar. Then finally he set her down on top of the bar, her feet swinging high off the floor.

He stood back for a moment, looking deep into her eyes, and Chloe could see that he was breathing raggedly—and she knew it had nothing to do with the effort of carrying her into the pool house. Her own heart was racing and she was trembling from head to foot.

Suddenly he stepped forward, pressing himself between her thighs, and cupped her face with his large hands. For once their mouths were the same height, and he drew closer and began to kiss her.

His tongue slid sensuously between her lips, in an erotic exploration that quickly left her breathless again. At the same time she felt him grip the hem of her T-shirt and she sat up taller, arching towards him as he peeled it off her. Her bra followed quickly, then his hands closed over her breasts, caressing and coaxing her nipples into diamond-hard points.

'Oh!' A moan of pleasure sighed out of her and her head fell backwards. Her hands rested flat on the surface of the bar just behind her, and her arms were locked straight, stabilising her body as she thrust her breasts towards him.

His tongue flicked over one erect nipple and she trembled in response, willing him to continue. Then he sucked the whole aching peak of her breast into his mouth and worked it with his tongue. The impact was immediate and she suddenly found herself rocking her pelvis, startled by the wildfire he had ignited in an entirely different part of her body.

A low, almost feral growl rumbled out of Lorenzo, as if he was completely in tune with what she was experiencing. His hands went straight to her jeans and undid the button, then moved quickly on to the zip. He struggled for a moment, cursing her jeans as he failed to unfasten them.

'Lie back!' he commanded, and Chloe found herself obeying. A moment later Lorenzo tugged the offending garment off, removing her underwear at the same time. She was about to sit up, but then he reached out and pushed her firmly back down.

Chloe drew in a shaky breath, realising that she was lying completely naked on the bar, with Lorenzo poised intimately between her legs. His breath was hot on her exposed centre and a rush of excitement surged through her, making her start to tremble uncontrollably.

The black granite bar was cold beneath the skin, but she was burning up with sexual anticipation. Then, when his mouth made contact with her pulsing flesh, she felt as if she'd gone up in flames.

The intensity of the sensation buzzing through her quivering body made her cry out. She could see the sky above her through the glass roof of the pool house, and it felt as if she had taken flight, spiralling up through the fluffy white clouds into the blue heavens.

She pressed her hands against the granite, trying instinctively to anchor herself, but his mouth continued to work its magic, sending her up and up, further and further out of her body. Time ceased to exist and there was nothing she could do but surrender to the incredible waves of pleasure rolling through her. Then just when she didn't know if she could bear the intensity any longer, the moment exploded into a starburst of euphoric bliss.

She lay panting on the bar, unable to move a muscle, feeling completely and utterly satisfied. Then the next thing she knew she was back in Lorenzo's arms. He carried her to the lounge area and laid her down on one of the couches.

She gazed up at him languidly, limp with the after-effects of her intense orgasm. But then, as he moved over her, a reawakened blast of sexual excitement tore through her body.

She'd never known it was possible to fly back to

such incredible heights so quickly, but as his hard, masculine length slid deep inside she cried out in pleasure.

Her whole being was suffused with glorious, undulating waves of rapture, and she closed her eyes, clinging to Lorenzo. His powerful body was hot and hard, and as he moved within her she sensed him begin to tremble and quake. Then, as he continued to thrust, driving them both on and on, they suddenly took flight together.

She felt him give one last mighty shudder as he reached his powerful climax, and at the same instant her own soul soared back into the heavens, as another explosion of ecstasy burst through her.

She cried out his name again and again, unaware that she was suddenly sobbing without restraint.

It was later that evening when Chloe drifted back to wakefulness. She was lying on the couch in the pool house, wearing a large, fluffy white robe that Lorenzo had wrapped around her after they had made love in the shower. Her body felt utterly relaxed, and was glowing with sensual fulfilment.

Her gaze settled on the dark windows and she realised with a jolt how late it was. She shot bolt upright, and saw Lorenzo coming towards her carrying a tray of food.

'Emma!' she gasped. 'What time is it?'

'She's safe with Mrs Guest,' Lorenzo said reassuringly as he put the tray on a low table and sat opposite her. 'She seems to have developed a soft spot for her. And also I believe she's already put her down for the night.'

'Oh,' Chloe said, sinking back on the couch. 'I can't believe it's so late. I must have slept a long time.'

Her hands moved instinctively to draw the robe tighter around her body. Then suddenly an unsettling wave of uncertainty washed over her as she remembered how completely she had surrendered herself to Lorenzo's lovemaking. How she had wept uncontrollably in his arms.

The whole experience had been absolutely mind-blowing—the most incredible hours of her life. Somehow she realised that everything was changed forever—that *she* was changed forever.

She was lost to Lorenzo, and she knew there was nothing she could do about it now.

'Mrs Guest sent some food over,' he said, his deep voice drawing her out of her thoughts. 'Apparently you've hardly touched your meals for the last twenty-four hours, and she wanted me to ensure that you ate something.'

Chloe gazed at him, struggling to focus on the commonplace content of his comment. Somehow it didn't seem right that they should be talking about eating after making such a life-altering decision, and sharing such an extraordinary level of intimacy.

'Are you hungry?' Lorenzo asked, leaning forward to remove the covers that were keeping the food fresh.

'I don't know,' Chloe said, gazing at the food without really seeing it.

She glanced up at him and saw that he was looking at her with a strangely intense expression on his face. Suddenly she got the impression that he knew how uncertain she was feeling. That he understood what a monumental step they had taken in their newly defined relationship.

Except he did not know how much Chloe still loved him. That was something that he couldn't— or wouldn't—understand. And something that, for the sake of her own protection, she did not want him to know.

'Start with something light,' Lorenzo said. 'Maybe some fruit.'

He leant forward to pass her a plate, then couldn't take his eyes off her as she reached out to take it.

The fluffy white sleeve of the robe fell back to reveal her slender wrist and a shot of sensual appreciation went through him.

God, he wanted her! Even after spending all afternoon revelling in her naked body—making love to her and sharing the most intimate secrets of her sexuality—just a glimpse of her wrist had him burning with desire once again.

His gaze followed her movements as she took a

bite of peach, and a blast of desire shot through him as her lips closed around the fruit and the column of her throat moved as she swallowed.

But for the moment he would content himself with watching her eat. Despite the lack of inhibition in their lovemaking that afternoon, he didn't think she was ready to play erotic games with food.

She had turned away slightly, as if she was uncomfortable under his scrutiny, and abruptly stopped eating, her hand poised halfway to her mouth.

'What is it?' he asked, unsettled by the appalled look on her face.

She turned to him, wide-eyed, all the colour abruptly drained from her face.

'We're in a glass-walled building,' she said hoarsely. 'This afternoon…oh, God…anyone could have seen.'

'No one saw anything,' Lorenzo reassured her. 'It's all privacy glass; you can't see in from outside. Even now,' he added, 'even now at night time with the lights on inside. We can swim naked and no one will see.'

'Really?' she asked. 'You're not just saying that?'

'Come outside with me, and see for yourself,' he suggested. 'But finish your meal first. You need to keep up your strength.'

CHAPTER SEVEN

'DO YOU want me to take you outside to try and look through the windows?' Lorenzo asked, some time later. 'Just to prove how private it is in here?'

'No, that's all right. I believe you.' Chloe looked at him, feeling a flush of warmth on her cheeks.

'You don't sound entirely convinced,' Lorenzo said. 'Are you worried you might not like what you find?'

'No,' she said. 'I like it in here, that's all. I'm comfortable where I am.'

She was telling the truth, but in her heart she knew there was more to it than that. They'd just spent a surprisingly relaxed hour or so together, eating the delicious food Mrs Guest had provided and chatting about inconsequential topics. It had felt safe and thoroughly normal—things that had been completely lacking in her life recently. She was half-afraid if she left the pool house the spell would be broken.

'In that case, how about taking a swim?' Lorenzo asked. 'No need to worry that you haven't got your costume.'

'I like it in my robe,' she said, ignoring the fluttering that started inside her at the thought of swimming naked in front of Lorenzo. 'I told you I was nice and comfy.'

She looked at him, letting her gaze run over his powerful body, and couldn't help smiling. He had put back on the same shirt and trousers that he'd been wearing when he found her beside the pond, but they were uncommonly crumpled for a man who usually seemed to look perfect without any effort.

'What are you smiling at?' he asked. 'I saw you giving me the once-over. Did you find something amusing?'

'You look a mess.' She laughed—then covered her mouth abruptly with her hand. It felt good to laugh, and she couldn't remember the last time she had done it.

'Hey!' Lorenzo surged off his seat and bore down on her with an indignant expression on his face, which rapidly turned blatantly sexual as he leant over her. 'At least I'm wearing my own clothes—perhaps I shouldn't have let you have that robe. I think I want it back.'

Chloe drew in a shaky breath and stared up at him with her stomach doing somersaults of anticipation.

He reached for the edges of the robe, and started to pull it open. In a moment he would reveal her bare, defenceless body.

Suddenly a rush of bold, wanton confidence flooded through her.

'You can have it back,' she said, ducking beneath his arms and jumping to her feet. 'I'm going for a swim after all.'

She walked quickly to the edge of the pool, glanced over her shoulder at his startled face and smiled mischievously. Then she tossed the robe away from her.

Lorenzo stared at her, his eyes gleaming with desire as his gaze ran up and down her naked back. But then his eyes narrowed with intent and he started moving towards her.

She laughed, enjoying the freedom of the sound as it echoed off the glass walls, and dived into the clear blue pool.

The water was deliciously cool against her naked body and she glided under the surface feeling as free as a dolphin. She came up for air halfway along the pool, then continued to swim as quickly as she could to the far end. There she rolled over onto her back, pushed off the wall and kicked languorously towards her starting point, where Lorenzo was standing.

She slowed right down, trying to catch her breath, and stared up at the ceiling. Suddenly she realised that she was looking at herself reflected in the glass, so clearly that she could have been looking into an enormous overhead mirror.

It was a strange feeling gazing up at herself, her arms and legs moving slowly, her body undulating gently in the water. She could see her breasts breaking through the surface—her nipples dark, rose-coloured buds against milky-white skin.

A wave of sexual awareness washed over her, lapping at her with the movement of the water. She knew Lorenzo was looking at her—seeing the same sight that she could see in the ceiling. Her naked limbs and exposed body—her bare breasts thrusting through the water.

The intense jolt of desire that suddenly shot through her left her light-headed with its intensity. She rolled over abruptly and stared up at Lorenzo.

He had stripped off his clothes and was standing naked beside the pool.

She gazed at him breathlessly—unable to drag her eyes away from his magnificent body. It was muscled and athletic—and entirely aroused.

The room suddenly closed in around them and she felt her pulse rate jump up another notch. Her tongue flicked out to moisten her lips and she pushed her dripping hair off her face, which suddenly felt burning hot.

Lorenzo stepped to the edge and dived in, barely making a splash. She gasped and stared down into the pool, struggling to see through the rippling surface, but almost at once he surged out of the water right in front of her. Her breath caught in her throat and a deluge of adrenaline buzzed through her veins. A millisecond later he had seized her in his arms and dragged her hard against his body.

Her feet didn't reach the floor, so she wrapped her legs instinctively around his waist. She could feel his erection nudging at her and another rush of arousal took hold of her, igniting a fire between her thighs and setting her whole body shaking.

They'd made love three times that afternoon, and each time had been as explosive and incredible as the first. It was hard to comprehend how much she still needed him—how much she wanted to feel him thrusting inside her.

She welcomed the all-encompassing, mind-blowing intensity of it, and she had no wish to take things slowly. In a shamelessly provocative movement, she clung to his shoulders to support herself, and slid her body sinuously against his, lowering herself until she felt the tip of his erection press against the pulsing centre of her desire.

A deep, almost animal sound of raw sexual need burst out of Lorenzo. She could feel his hot explosion of breath on her neck where she had bowed her head against his shoulder.

Suddenly his mouth closed bruisingly over the sensitive skin beneath her ear. He kissed her hard, working his way down the side of her neck, massaging with his tongue and nibbling with his teeth.

She closed her eyes and heard herself moaning with a build-up of raw sexual need. Her heart was racing, sending the blood pulsing through her veins, dilating her senses and making her almost unbearably aware of the silken steel of his arousal pressing against her own throbbing flesh.

She writhed against him, willing him to take her. She had to feel him inside her, filling her with hard, thrusting rapture once more. It was impossible for her to wait any longer, and she moved again, aligning herself with his erection, and pressed down onto him.

His wonderful, hard length slid deep inside her, and a moan of momentary satisfaction escaped her. But then his hands were on her waist and he was lifting her, disconnecting their bodies, pulling away and leaving her flesh empty and pulsating with unfulfilled need.

'Not yet.' The tortured sound of his voice raked across her senses, matching the level of frustration she was feeling. 'Unless you've changed your mind— we need protection.'

Understanding flashed through her mind, but she was too turned on to feel any relief. Lorenzo was already moving towards the side of the pool, carrying her with him, she still clinging to him in the same intimate position.

He sat down on the wide steps and lowered her carefully, so that she was straddling him with her knees resting on either side of him. Then he turned and reached for a condom packet, which he had left ready beside the pool.

Chloe looked down at his marvellous physique. His powerful legs were hot beneath her thighs and the muscles on his chest and stomach rippled beneath his golden skin as he moved. But her eyes were drawn to his arousal, and just looking sent another surge of excitement through her own body.

Suddenly she found herself slipping off his lap and leaning forward to take him in her mouth. She closed her lips around his powerful shaft and she sensed his body kick with pleasure. He felt smooth and hot under her tongue, and her eyelids slid down as she gave herself over entirely to the experience of bringing him pleasure.

Lorenzo stared up at the glass ceiling, almost overwhelmed by the exquisite sensations Chloe was imparting with her mouth. He could see them both reflected above, and the sight of her slender body bowed over his, her head moving in synchrony with the jolts of pleasure rocketing through his body, was almost too much.

'No more.' His voice was hoarse and nearly unrecognisable as his hands went to her shoulders to lift her away.

She raised her head shakily and he could see in

her eyes that she was as turned on as he was. He reached for the foil packet with trembling hands and was glad when she took it and tore it open. Together they rolled the condom onto his erect flesh. Then, never breaking eye contact, she straddled him once more.

Chloe gazed dizzily into his eyes, gripped by a final rush of anticipation. Unable to wait another moment, she lowered herself down onto him, filling her aching body with him. Then suddenly her strength gave out and her thighs were shaking too much to hold her weight.

She closed her eyes again, revelling in the heat of him embedded deeply inside her, but desperate to feel him move. Then, as if he had read her mind, Lorenzo hauled them both out of the water as one and laid her down beside the pool. Her discarded towelling robe was beneath her, cushioning her from the hard floor, but it scarcely mattered, as all she was aware of was the glorious feel of Lorenzo thrusting inside her.

Her breath was coming in shallow gasps and the thrilling wildfire was building rapidly within her again. She could hear Lorenzo's ragged breathing, and her last coherent thought was how amazing it was that they could bring each other such extraordinary pleasure.

But then the rhythm of his fluid thrusts increased and she arched up to meet him. Every movement he made engulfed her with blazing sensation and carried her higher, up into a realm that was filled only with wave upon wave of unbelievable delight. Then when she reached a fever pitch of almost unbearable intensity, he pushed her further still, until suddenly she shot into orgasm with an unrestrained cry of rapture.

Her body convulsed with pleasure, tightening around him, driving him on to his own moment of release. Then they collapsed together, gasping for breath as they slowly drifted back down to earth.

The following morning Chloe woke up in the bedroom. At some point during the night Lorenzo must have carried her back into the house, but she had been so soundly asleep that she had not noticed.

For a moment she felt sad that the magical interlude in the pool house was over, but the next second she heard Emma stirring in her cot beside the bed. Suddenly she realised that she'd missed the baby—she'd been too distracted over the past day or so to really connect with her.

As wonderful as the hours she'd spent shut away from the world with Lorenzo had been, it was good to be back where she belonged—although as soon as that thought passed through her mind, she found herself feeling surprised at it. So much had happened in the last twenty-four hours.

'Good morning.' Lorenzo's husky voice coming

from the doorway to the en suite took her by surprise. He was already showered and dressed informally in black trousers and a grey sweater.

'Hello.' She looked up at him and smiled shyly—appreciating the gorgeous sight of him in the form-fitting sweater, but suddenly embarrassed by the complete lack of restraint she had shown the night before.

'I hope I didn't wake you,' Lorenzo said. 'I was hoping you would sleep in. I've got some arrangements I must make now, but I'd like to see you later this morning.'

He strode across to the bed and bent down to kiss her on the lips. Then he was gone.

Chloe lifted her fingers and pressed them lightly to her lips. She couldn't believe how much had changed so quickly.

Later that morning Chloe was outside with Emma. It was another fine day and the garden was lovely. As she looked around Chloe realised it was that special time of year when everything in nature was at its most verdant and fresh. The delicate new leaves had not long unfurled and the grass was a lush emerald swathe.

She felt so much better than she had the previous day. So much more hopeful for the future.

She had promised Liz that she would not batten down her heart, and she was glad that she had kept her word. Things with Lorenzo seemed wonderful. He had been considerate and caring. And he'd understood her concerns about rushing into starting a family—he'd even been the one to make them pause long enough to use protection on the occasion when Chloe had let herself get carried away on the moment.

It was true that Lorenzo continued to insist that he didn't believe in love, but Chloe found it increasingly hard to comprehend. His actions seemed loving. In fact, up until their wedding day, his actions had always seemed loving.

Chloe shook her head. She didn't understand— and she didn't want to think about it. She had promised Liz that she would think happy thoughts.

A movement caught her eye and she looked over her shoulder to see Lorenzo coming towards them across the lawn.

'Come inside and pack your bags,' he said. 'I've arranged a holiday for us. Somewhere far away with no memories or associations, where you can truly relax and recuperate.'

'Oh,' Chloe gazed at him in surprise—although it wasn't the first time he'd made a similar announcement. When they were together he was always whisking her away on exotic or romantic breaks. 'Where are we going? Is it somewhere suitable for babies—not a wooden hut on a deserted island a thousand miles from the nearest doctor?'

'Mauritius,' he said. 'Rest assured, it's perfectly civilised. We'll fly overnight and be at the hotel in time for breakfast. And, as it happens, Mrs Guest's daughter, Lucy, is a qualified nursery nurse. She'll be coming with us, to make sure you really do rest and relax.'

CHAPTER EIGHT

CHLOE sat enjoying a leisurely breakfast on their private balcony, at the exclusive hotel Lorenzo had brought them to in Mauritius. The giant suite of rooms he'd booked occupied a corner location, and in one direction she had an impressive view of the hotel's stunning gardens and in the other direction the tropical water of the Indian Ocean glittered in the bright sunshine.

She had forgotten to eat for the past few minutes, being completely captivated by the industrious efforts of a weaverbird that was building a nest not far from where she sat.

First it flew up to the palm tree right next to where Chloe was sitting. It gripped the edge of the frond in its beak and flew downwards, tearing off a strip as it did so. Then, a long ribbon of palm leaf fluttering behind it, the little bird flew to its nest, which was dangling down from a branch on another nearby tree. It was a bit too far away for Chloe to see just how it went about weaving the nest, and she was wishing she had some binoculars, when a familiar voice startled her out of her observations.

'Good morning, Chloe,' Lorenzo drawled, his voice still husky from another night of lovemaking. He pulled up a chair to join her and reached for a glass of orange juice.

'Good morning,' Chloe replied, feeling her heart skip a beat and a blush rise to her cheeks. They'd spent one night in Mauritius and it was the first time they'd made love in a bed since they'd been back together, but it had been just as incredible as all the times in the pool house. 'I've been watching a weaverbird.'

'It's the male that builds the nest, you know,' Lorenzo said, not missing a beat. 'Then he has to wait to see if the female will approve of it or destroy it.'

'Really? I've seen them on TV, but never in real life before,' Chloe said, thinking about all the effort the male had to make, never knowing if there would be a positive outcome for him.

Although it was the bird's natural instinct, she was suddenly struck by what an extraordinary act of faith that was.

It was just like life, she thought, remembering the promise she had made to Liz. There were no guarantees that things would turn out the way she hoped, but without faith and commitment she risked never finding what she searched for.

'Anyway, you'd better get ready,' Lorenzo said, taking her by surprise and standing up briskly. 'I'll be back in ten minutes. I've got a boat to take us along the coast—there's something I want to show you.'

The speedboat slowed and turned into the mouth of a wide, lazy river. Chloe had enjoyed the trip along the coast. She loved the stiff sea breeze blowing her hair and the exciting bob and bounce as the boat sped along.

The stunning beauty of the coastline had thrilled her. The pure white beaches edged with swaying palms and casuarinas, the amazing turquoise water of the lagoon and the deep blue sea out beyond the coral reef took her breath away.

At least she told herself that was the cause of her erratic heartbeat and the difficulty she was having breathing normally. It had nothing to do with Lorenzo sitting so close, his arm along the back of the seat behind her shoulders.

Emma had stayed at the hotel, with Mrs Guest's daughter, Lucy, so the only thing holding her attention was Lorenzo.

'It's so quiet,' Chloe said, pleased by how level her voice sounded. She leant forward to look over the edge of the boat. 'The river's very deep. Are those dark shadows down there rocks?'

'Yes,' Lorenzo said. 'Larger boats can't go very far upriver because of them.'

'It's incredible,' she said, looking around at the scenery. It was startlingly different from the glittering turquoise sea and white sand she had grown accustomed to back at the hotel and on their trip along the coast.

The water was very deep and flowed so slowly that the surface was smooth like a dark green mirror reflecting the lush green growth on either side of the river. The banks themselves were made of massive grey-brown boulders rising high above the water. 'I feel like I've stepped into an adventure, going up the Amazon into uncharted territory or something.'

'It is beautiful,' Lorenzo agreed, 'but hardly uncharted. We've come early to have the place to ourselves for a while.'

Chloe glanced at the driver of the boat and at Lorenzo's personal bodyguard, who was also with them. They weren't really alone, and she found herself feeling disappointed.

'What's that noise?' Chloe asked suddenly as the faint but unmistakable sound of rushing water reached her ears.

'Can you guess?' Lorenzo asked, his playful grin flashing in a way that made butterflies flutter in her stomach. It was wonderful to see him like this—it was almost as if they were back to their early days of dating, before so many horrible things had happened.

'A waterfall?' Chloe asked in delight. All her life

she had loved waterfalls, being completely entranced by their beauty, power and romance.

The boat wound its way slowly up the river, the driver expertly manoeuvring between the great boulders that hid just beneath the surface.

'Wow!' Chloe breathed as the boat moved past a particularly large rock and the waterfall came into view. 'It's beautiful.'

She stared in awe at the mass of white water pouring down over a sheer drop into the river in front of them. She could feel moisture rising up from the foaming water, refreshing her warm skin.

'Come on,' Lorenzo said, holding out his hand to her as the boat pulled up to a rocky ledge. 'We can climb up and swim at the top.'

The mention of swimming sent a tingle of excitement thrilling through her. A vivid memory of the last time they swam played out in her mind.

'Is it safe?' Chloe found herself asking the first thing that came to her, although really she knew she could trust Lorenzo with her safety.

'Of course,' he said mildly.

The driver had jumped out and was holding the boat steady and Lorenzo spoke in swift Italian to his bodyguard.

'Follow me,' Lorenzo instructed. 'It's easy.'

For a moment Chloe paused, letting her eyes drink in the masculine beauty that was Lorenzo Valente—her husband. He was wearing casual shorts and a skin-tight black T-shirt that showed off his sculpted body to perfection.

His vibrant blue eyes sparkled, making the intense colour of the tropical sky fade into insignificance. And his golden skin glowed with a vitality that took her breath away and suddenly made her want to run the tip of her tongue up the strong column of his throat.

She bit her lip and ducked her head to hide her blazing cheeks. Something in his expression had made her pulse quicken—as if he was about to take her to a place where they could make love. At that moment it was exactly what she wanted him to do.

'Let's go,' she said, amazed how level she kept her voice considering the somersaults of sensual expectation her stomach was performing.

She followed Lorenzo across and up the rocks. It was an easy climb but it needed all her concentration. It would be too easy to slip. At the top she turned and realised that they were alone. Both the boat driver and the bodyguard had stayed with the boat.

'All right?' Lorenzo asked, letting his gaze linger longer than necessary on the quick rise and fall of Chloe's breasts. 'It's quite a steep climb.'

'Yes, thank you,' Chloe replied, knowing that her rapid breathing was caused more by the realisation that she was alone with Lorenzo and the look in his eyes than by the exertion of the climb.

He led her forward onto a large flat expanse of rock. On their left they looked down at the waterfall from above, the gushing white water truly stunning with the sunlight sparkling on it.

'It's really beautiful,' Chloe said in a quiet voice, gazing at the fine mist of water droplets surrounding the waterfall and the colourful rainbows that arched around it.

'Yes, I'm still very impressed, even though I've seen it before.'

Lorenzo's voice was loaded with sexual intensity and Chloe knew he wasn't really talking about the waterfall. She held her breath and kept her face turned firmly away from him. She felt the flutter of anticipation start to rise in her stomach again and she wanted to make the moment last.

'I've always loved rivers,' she said slightly breathlessly. 'And especially waterfalls.'

'I remember,' Lorenzo said, taking her by surprise. 'You told me about that river with giant boulder stepping stones that you loved as a child when you went on holiday in Devon.'

'Oh…yes,' Chloe stammered, feeling even more shaky. She couldn't remember telling Lorenzo that, but then they had talked about so many things since she started working for him, and especially since they started dating.

'And you told me about your walking holidays in the Lake District, where you and your sister went in search of anything labelled *force*—meaning waterfall—on your map.'

'You've got a good memory,' Chloe said uncomfortably. She could have sworn she remembered every single second of their time together, remembered every single word they'd ever said to each other. It made her uneasy to realise she was mistaken.

'You don't recall our conversation,' Lorenzo said. His eyes narrowed as he studied her face.

'Of course I do.' Chloe startled herself by lying. She didn't like the sudden feeling that Lorenzo had her at a disadvantage.

'No, you don't,' Lorenzo said emphatically. A half-smile was playing at his lips but it didn't reach his eyes. 'Sit down and catch your breath.'

'I can climb up a few rocks without needing to sit down!' Chloe exclaimed.

'It doesn't matter that you can't remember.' Lorenzo's voice was quiet now, but his eyes still burned dangerously.

'Even you can't remember every single word that was said,' Chloe said huffily.

'Yes, I can,' said Lorenzo lightly, lowering himself down onto a large flat rock with a deep pool in front of it. 'Every single word. Now, sit down here with me.'

Chloe tossed her head, and looked away sideways at the rushing water of the river. She had the unnerving feeling that Lorenzo would take this as evidence that she had never paid full attention to him.

That this was the explanation behind why she had made such a terrible mistake in her expectations of their marriage.

But that was different, she told herself. Forgetting a few inconsequential conversations about family holidays, which had probably taken place during her hectic working day while she was juggling the duties of an exacting job and demanding boss, did *not* mean she would have forgotten something so important as whether he explained fully that he wanted a loveless marriage of convenience.

She took a deep breath and sat down on the rock next to Lorenzo. She'd been alone with him for no more that a few minutes and already her emotions were all over the place again. Things might be wonderful between them when they were making love— but this proved that there were still massive cracks in their relationship.

'Is that where people swim?' she asked, carefully avoiding meeting his eye. Instead she looked at the deep, inviting pool, which was in front of them, surrounded by smooth brown rocks. 'The water certainly looks cool. Does it come down from the mountains?'

'I valued every minute I spent with you,' Lorenzo said, ignoring her attempted change of subject. 'Our conversations ranged over so many topics. I was impressed by your enthusiasm for life, your honesty, the way you expressed yourself so freely and openly.'

'Is that why you tricked me into a loveless marriage?'

The words were out before Chloe fully realised what she was saying. Lorenzo had just told her something wonderful—something that should have made her heart glad. And yet she'd thrown his gesture back in his face.

A furious change came over him and he surged to his feet. Suddenly he was stripping off his T-shirt and kicking away his canvas shoes.

'I'm sorry—' she started, but the look he threw at her over his shoulder quelled her apology before she had gone any further.

'Save it!' he snapped, before turning his back on her and diving into the deep natural pool. His long, powerful strokes bore him rapidly away across the water, and Chloe knew that her unintentionally caustic comment had angered him.

She stood and stared into the water. A couple of minutes ago it had looked inviting, but now that Lorenzo was pounding his way back in her direction she found herself trembling.

'Come in with me!' he commanded, tossing his wet hair out of his eyes with a fierce gesture.

Chloe hesitated, reluctant to join him. He looked

completely in his element, surrounded by the majestic power and grace of the river as it carved its way through the ancient volcanic rock. But he was emanating an untamed savage energy that suddenly frightened her as much as it excited her.

'It doesn't look safe,' she said, taking a step back from the edge. 'What stops you getting washed over the waterfall?'

'There's hardly any current this side of those big rocks,' Lorenzo said impatiently. 'As long as we stay this side it is safe. You know I wouldn't have brought you anywhere dangerous.'

Chloe drew her lower lip into her mouth, undecided. It looked like an incredible place to swim—but she was nervous both of the elemental power of the river and of Lorenzo's intense mood.

Then she remembered her promise to Liz. She might never get an opportunity like this again and she would be foolish to let it slip by. In her heart she knew Lorenzo would never put her at real risk.

She stripped off her own blouse and light summer skirt to reveal her bikini, then slid off the rock into the water. She felt herself tremble slightly and released the breath she hadn't known she'd been holding.

'Follow me,' Lorenzo said, beckoning to her as he swam away.

Chloe followed him without speaking as he led her across the pool. The water was cool, but pleasantly energising, and her body was already starting to buzz in expectation of Lorenzo's lovemaking—for she was certain that he was leading her to a place where he could make love to her.

They made their way around the bend in the river by a combination of swimming across deep water and climbing over the giant boulders that rose up beneath them. Chloe loved every minute of it. The setting was absolutely beautiful, and the knowledge that she would soon be in Lorenzo's arms heightened her pleasure.

'We're here,' Lorenzo said at last, and Chloe stopped and stared in wonder at the sight of a whole array of shallow rocky basins fed by smaller, gentler waterfalls.

'It's amazing,' she breathed, unbelievably grateful that she had followed Lorenzo and not given in to her anxieties.

'The locals come here for a water massage,' Lorenzo said, moving away from her towards one of the smaller waterfalls. 'They call it natural hydrotherapy.'

He flashed her a broad smile that showed no hint that he was still angry with her, then pushed himself backwards under the flow of a small waterfall.

Chloe stared in horrified shock as water poured down over him, plastering his black hair to his bowed head and sheeting over his body. She knew he was strong and fit, but her heart started to pound as she looked at him standing under the water.

Being pummelled by gallons of water rushing over a rocky outcrop was not her idea of a massage. It looked frankly terrifying.

'Stop it!' she shouted. 'Get out of there!' But the sound of the crashing water obliterated her cries, and Lorenzo showed no sign of moving.

She lurched forward to grab him, but water poured down over her face and into her eyes, blinding her. She flailed wildly, reaching out to him and calling his name. Then suddenly her fists came into contact with the solid muscle of his chest and she pounded him angrily—not caring whether she hurt him, just wanting him to stop his silly, dangerous game in the torrential waterfall.

The next second she felt his hands close like steel clamps on her arms, and he lifted her back out of the deluge of water.

'What are you doing?' he demanded, holding her steady as she scrubbed sodden hair out of her eyes and spat river water out of her mouth. 'This is not a leisure centre with a lifeguard watching out for us! You can't mess about like that—you must have respect for the power of natural forces.'

'I'm not the one messing about!' she cried, lashing out at him again. 'Why did you have to do that? I thought you'd brought me here to make love to me—not to scare me to death!'

Lorenzo was staring at her, clearly shocked by the vehemence of her attack on him. There was a puzzled look on his face—as if he couldn't understand what she was frightened of.

'It's all right.' He reached for her, but she stepped back out of his grasp.

'Why would you take such a risk?' she demanded. 'I couldn't bear it if—'

She stopped abruptly—suddenly not willing to reveal her feelings to him. He'd already belittled her too many times for that.

'If what?' he asked. 'What were you talking about?'

'Nothing,' she said, splashing away from him in the chest-deep water. 'I'm going back to the boat.'

'Wait.' He moved quicker than her, and the next second his hands closed around her waist. 'I thought you just said you wanted to make love.'

'Let me go!' she gasped, but he pulled her back against his body, lifting her feet off the bottom of the pool. She wriggled in his arms, but she had her back to him and there was nothing she could get hold of.

'That feels good,' he said, rocking his hips forwards so that the hard heat of his arousal nudged against the curve of her bottom. 'I like your idea to make love.'

An answering rush of desire stormed through Chloe, almost making her forget that she was angry with him. But she did not like the way he was manhandling her—even though it was turning her on faster that she would have thought possible.

'It wasn't my idea,' she said, ignoring the liquid heat that was beginning to pool deep inside her as he rocked his pelvis against her once more. 'I said that I thought that was why you'd brought me here.'

'No.' He spoke directly against her ear, his breath hot on her skin. 'I thought you'd like to see the waterfall.'

'Then why is there a condom in your pocket?' she asked in exasperation, reaching behind her to run her hand over his shorts.

It was a mistake. Her palm collided with the hard shaft of his erection straining against the fabric and another rush of arousal shot through her.

'That is for you,' he murmured throatily. 'Now, lie still and let me see what I can do to please you.'

'No…' The world formed silently on Chloe's lips, but she didn't mean it. His hands were moving over her body beneath the water, setting off a chain reaction that she was powerless to resist.

He stepped backwards through the water, pulling her with him, until he was leaning against the rock. He was firmly balanced and could support her easily while his hands ran lightly all over her body.

A deep series of tremors started to quiver through her, and she reached out instinctively to steady herself, but there was nothing to grab on to.

'Trust me,' he murmured in her ear. 'Just let your limbs float free and trust me to hold you.'

His voice was mesmerising and Chloe found

herself automatically doing as he instructed. She leant back into him so that her back was against his chest and her head was resting on his shoulder—and she let her arms and legs hover naturally in the water, finding their own balance.

He traced his hands over her body, his fingertips lightly teasing with gentle swirling patterns that echoed the gentle wash of the water over her skin. She was aware when he tugged at her bikini strings, but she didn't move, and made no effort to stop the tiny scraps of fabric floating away.

She liked feeling naked in the river pool, with his hands and the rippling water caressing every part of her body without hindrance.

Slowly he began to touch her more intimately, teasing her with a delicate touch on her breast or a gentle brush between her legs.

She began to tremble, but she trusted him completely. She knew he wouldn't let her slip, so she just floated in the water, letting the sensations ripple through her.

He started to concentrate his caresses on her breasts, and she felt her breathing deepen. Her body was rocking naturally in the water, rising slightly as she breathed in, so that her nipples broke through the surface, and sinking back down as she exhaled. The sensation it created was exquisite, almost as if his caresses were multiplied by every drop of water flowing over her skin.

'Look down at your body,' Lorenzo breathed in her ear. 'Your breasts are so beautiful.'

Obediently she opened her eyes. Her skin looked so pale in the water, and Lorenzo's hands were rich golden-brown as they moved across her body. And somehow, as she watched her body rise and fall, the sensations he was creating were enhanced.

She began to tremble harder, feeling little darts of pleasure coiling through her body from her breasts deep down through her body. His hands slid to her waist to steady her, but the next thing she knew one hand had moved straight down between her legs.

But this time he didn't brush her lightly, teasing her with delicate touches. This time his fingers went straight for the pulsing centre of her desire.

'Oh!' she cried out in startled pleasure as he began to caress her with direct intent. The games he had played earlier, teasing and tempting with gentle strokes, were over. Now he was focused on stimulating her in the most effective way he knew how.

It only took seconds before her body was writhing with overwhelming, building sensation. One hand closed over her breast, massaging and rolling her nipple, and the other stayed firmly between her legs, sending pulsing waves of sheer pleasure shooting through her entire being.

She felt as if she was taking flight. Her whole body was inflamed with pure sexual rapture. She had never reached orgasm so quickly, and a distant part of her mind could not quite believe it. But then she shot up into the heights of ecstasy like a rocket into space.

For long moments she arched back against Lorenzo, her whole body clenched in the throes of release. Then she relaxed, trembling in the glorious aftermath, and let herself continue to float.

A little while later she felt Lorenzo turning her. His arms slipped under her and he lifted her out of the water and laid her on a smooth brown rock. She sank down into the sun-warmed surface, feeling utterly spent, her arms spread wide and her legs relaxed and soft.

She was absolutely naked and lying spread out in the tropical sun without a care in the world. She closed her eyes and drifted off into a state of dreamy bliss.

Lorenzo sat beside her, looking down at her gorgeous body. She was absolutely exquisite. Her pale skin was glowing with almost ethereal beauty next to the deep brown of the rock and her hair was spread out in a golden halo around her head.

He was still so turned on that it hurt, and soon he would rouse her again, knowing he could easily bring her back to incredible heights of pleasure, while he found his own release. But right then he couldn't get enough of simply looking at her.

He loved giving her pleasure. And he particularly

loved bringing her to orgasm. Whether he took it slow, teasing out each and every nuance of her ascent, or whether he sent her sky-rocketing with a few skilled caresses, there had never been another woman in his life that he had taken so much pleasure from pleasing.

And soon he would start the process again. She was gloriously relaxed and uninhibited, which was often an incredible starting point.

He shifted his position and pulled off his shorts so that he was naked too. Then rolled a condom onto his erect penis. There would be no interruptions—this time he would take them both to the point of rapture.

CHAPTER NINE

THE sparkling azure water of the Indian Ocean stretched out in front of Chloe as far as the eye could see. In fact she knew from reading her guidebook that there were over a thousand miles of glittering ocean between the island of Mauritius, where they were staying, and the east coast of Africa.

She could hardly believe how beautiful the palm-fringed beach was. Gentle waves were lapping on the white powder sand and, out across the clear turquoise water of the lagoon, she could see a line of white water where impressive breakers were crashing into the coral reef.

She sat comfortably on her sun lounger, holding Emma on her lap while she searched through her bag looking for the sunblock.

'May I join you?' Lorenzo's silky Italian accent purred against her ear, catching her unawares, and a shiver prickled across her skin despite the heat of the tropical sun.

Her body was still humming from their amazing lovemaking at the waterfall that morning. She couldn't imagine how Lorenzo had been able to switch from that experience to spending the last couple of hours sending emails and making work phone calls.

'Of course,' she smiled, her breath catching in her throat as she turned to face him.

He looked incredible, she thought, wearing a tight black singlet that revealed altogether too much of his powerfully muscled shoulders and a pair of black shorts that showed off his strong, sexy legs.

'How is Emma?' he asked, taking the lounger next to them.

He leant back on his elbows so that his head was in the shade and stretched his long, bronzed legs out in front of him in the sun.

'Very well,' she said, looking down at him stretched out beside her. There was a funny sensation in the pit of her stomach—it was the first time he had ever asked after the baby. 'Although I can't seem to find the sunblock and I thought it was time for another coat, even though we're sitting in the shade.'

'Another pale English beauty,' he said. 'Tell me what I'm looking for, and I'll go back inside and bring you what you need.'

'Thanks, but it would be easier for me to fetch it,' Chloe said, lifting Emma up into her arms. 'I'm not entirely sure where it is. I may have lost it, in which case I'll pop to the hotel shop and buy some more.'

She tugged the baby's sunhat down snugly to shade her face, slipped her sunglasses on top of her head, and was just about to step out from under the large thatched parasol, when Lorenzo spoke.

'Then leave Emma with me,' he said.

Chloe paused, surprised by Lorenzo's suggestion. It was the first time he'd ever shown any inclination to be left alone with the baby.

Suddenly she realised she'd hesitated too long, and she glanced at him, startled to see her face reflected in the lenses of his sunglasses. She drew in a deep breath and pulled her own sunglasses down from on top of her head, hoping he had not read what was on her mind from the expression in her eyes.

Then she realised he was watching her reaction, and she felt her cheeks redden with embarrassment. The last thing she wanted was for him to think she did not trust him with the baby.

'All right,' she said, stepping back towards Lorenzo.

She started to chatter to Emma awkwardly, trying to cover up her delay in handing her over by beginning the stream of one-way conversation she usually maintained to keep the baby girl's attention.

'I'm just popping back inside,' she said to the infant. 'I won't be long. You go to Lorenzo…'

All at once her voice dried up. Calling him

Lorenzo had sounded wrong. But she couldn't call him Daddy—he was not Emma's father.

When Liz had asked Chloe to care for her daughter, she'd told her that she wanted Emma to call her Mummy, just like any other adopted child would refer to their adoptive mother. Then Chloe would use her judgement to decide when to tell her adopted daughter about her natural mother.

But Lorenzo had approached the adoption from an altogether different angle. Chloe had no idea what his thoughts on the subject were.

'Come to Daddy,' Lorenzo said, reaching out his arms to take the baby from Chloe.

'I'm sorry…' she started to say. 'I didn't know what—'

'Emma's biological father is not part of her life,' Lorenzo said flatly. 'I am the only father Emma will ever know and she will call *me* Daddy. No child growing up under my roof will be made to feel different from any other.'

A sudden swelling of emotion filled Chloe. She'd been concerned that Lorenzo had not truly accepted Emma. She believed he would always provide for her and do what he saw as the right thing. But she had worried that Emma would grow up knowing she was not the same as Lorenzo's natural children.

'That's good,' she said, knowing that it sounded inadequate in the circumstances—but she didn't want to make a big deal out of it. She was glad she was wearing sunglasses so that Lorenzo could not see the tears suddenly sparkling in her eyes. 'I know you don't want Emma to feel unloved…' She hesitated again, struggling to finish her comment smoothly. She hadn't meant to stumble into that other minefield—the discussion of love. 'I mean unwanted.'

'*Unloved* is the correct word,' Lorenzo said. 'No child growing up in my family will feel unloved.'

He reached up and took Emma decisively from Chloe's arms.

It was clear from his manner that he considered the conversation over—but Chloe did not mind. As far as she was concerned they had just made a massive step forward.

That evening Chloe and Lorenzo watched a display of the *séga,* the high-spirited and colourful national dance of Mauritius. It had been Chloe's idea—they had spent so much time alone together, mostly making love, that she was beginning to feel slightly detached from reality.

The dance was beautiful and compelling. The pulsating rhythm of the drums filled the air, and the dancers swirled and undulated without restraint. But as Chloe sat at a table with Lorenzo, watching him tap out the infectious beat with his fingers, she was beginning to think that what she really needed was to go home.

'You've had your hair cut.' He lifted his hand to touch Chloe's sleekly styled bob. 'I like it,' he added, tracing his fingers lightly over her newly exposed neck.

'Thank you.' She trembled as he caressed her sensitive skin. She was wearing a strapless dress and she felt his eyes settle on her naked shoulders.

'I don't recall noticing those freckles before,' he said, leaning closer so that she could feel his breath on the skin of her shoulders. 'Did the sun bring them out, like the ones on your face?'

'I don't know,' Chloe replied as the touch of his warm breath sent a delicious shiver quivering down her spine.

'You have beautiful skin—I adore your freckles.' He brushed his thumb lightly over her cheek.

'I ran out of foundation.' As soon as she spoke, it seemed a silly thing to say and she felt herself start to blush.

'I wondered why I noticed your freckles more,' he said, leaning forward to drop a feather-light kiss on her cheek.

'I think it's time to go home,' Chloe said, looking deep into his blue eyes.

'Of course.' He stood up immediately and led her out of the door into the hotel's lovely garden, which was their preferred route back towards their suite of rooms.

A warm, scented breeze brushed across Chloe's

skin and she could hear the gentle sound of the ocean. She looked up to see the palm trees swaying against an inky black sky studded with twinkling stars. It really was a beautiful place—a true tropical paradise. But she knew Lorenzo had misunderstood her request.

'No, I mean *really* go home,' she said, turning and catching both his hands in hers. 'I'm grateful for this wonderful holiday—but it's time to go back home and get on with our lives.'

One day almost two weeks later, Chloe stood on the *palazzo*'s main balcony overlooking the Grand Canal, holding Emma in her arms. She was chatting to the baby, pointing out the various boats that went past on the water—and keeping out of Lorenzo's way.

Things between them had become strained again and, apart from at night, when they continued to make love, she'd spent very little time with him. She thought that might be part of the reason she'd found it much harder to settle in to life in Venice than she had expected.

But the main reason for her disquiet was that almost every day she had found herself thinking about the devastating argument she'd had with Lorenzo on their wedding day—and him swearing that he did not believe in love.

In fact, virtually every room in the *palazzo* held

memories for her, and now as she looked back she found herself second-guessing everything that had ever been said and done between Lorenzo and herself.

If she'd been so wrong about the one thing that mattered the most—what else had not been as it seemed?

'I wonder where Daddy is now?' she said to Emma.

Since they'd been back in Venice he always seemed to be working—either at his offices or locked up in his study, or occasionally striding around the *palazzo* talking rapidly into his mobile phone, which was exactly what he was doing now.

She found it disconcerting to hear him bearing down on her while firing away in a language she still didn't fully understand—especially when spoken quickly by locals. The Venetian dialect seemed particularly impossible to learn.

She hugged Emma to her and listened carefully, trying to ascertain if Lorenzo was close. It was not that she was afraid to bump into him—it was just that she remembered from when she worked for him that if he was talking and striding like this, it probably meant he was in a bad mood.

'I'm here.' Lorenzo's deep voice coming from right behind her made her catch her breath. 'Did you want me for something?'

'Oh!' Chloe gasped, turning to see him stepping

out onto the broad balcony with her. 'No, not really. I heard your voice and I was just chatting to Emma. I've been showing her the boats on the Grand Canal.'

'Isn't she a little young for that?' Lorenzo asked, staring at her with a crease between his black brows.

'No,' Chloe responded, suppressing her irritation at the way Lorenzo was studying the baby—as if she were a strange little being of some kind. Not at all as if she was his adopted daughter. 'It's always good to chatter to babies, even if they are too young to understand. That's how they learn things.'

She pressed her teeth into her lower lip and looked at him, starting to worry that, despite his good intentions, he was having difficulty accepting another man's child into his home. The brief flash of interest he had shown in Emma that one particular afternoon on the beach in Mauritius had not been repeated, and he'd never made even the slightest effort to make a connection with the baby.

'I have something for her in my study,' he suddenly surprised Chloe by saying.

'Really?' she said, feeling a tiny spark of relief. She hoped that she'd been wrong, and that Lorenzo's aloofness had been no more than overwork. He'd taken a lot of time off to be with them, both in England and then in Mauritius. No doubt he had a good deal of work to catch up on. 'What is it?'

'I'm not entirely sure,' he said. 'Perhaps you should come with me and see for yourself.'

'That would be lovely,' Chloe said, feeling a little confused that he didn't know what the item was, but infusing her voice with warmth. If Lorenzo had made a kind gesture, she wanted him to know it was appreciated.

He set off through the *palazzo* at his usual great pace, as if he'd forgotten he was walking with Chloe, whose stride was considerably shorter. She wasn't prepared to run with the baby in her arms, so almost immediately she fell behind.

Lorenzo stopped and looked round, then glanced at his wristwatch.

'I have a conference call in a few minutes,' he said. 'Let me carry the baby, or we'll be out of time.'

Chloe handed Emma to him with a funny feeling inside. It rankled that Lorenzo only wanted to hold Emma to speed things up. But then, Chloe told herself, he had to start somewhere. If making a connection with Emma didn't come naturally for Lorenzo, then maybe it could grow from small, insignificant incidents.

He led the way to his study with Chloe half running to keep up. But when they got there he turned and abruptly passed Emma back to her.

'This is it.' He picked up a package from the floor behind his desk. 'Francesco Grazzini sent it. He's a business associate of mine,' he added, as if Chloe

didn't already know that. But she held her tongue—
that was not something worth starting an argument
over.

'Thank you.' She smiled tightly, knowing she
hadn't really managed to hide her deflated mood.

'What's wrong?' Lorenzo said, looking at her
sharply.

'Nothing.' She looked back at him, biting her lip
in indecision. Perhaps she should say something.
But then she remembered the conference call he
had mentioned—now was not the right time to get
into a potentially tricky conversation with him. 'I'll
leave you to your work.'

Lorenzo watched her hurry away out of his study
carrying the baby in her arms. She'd forgotten to
take Grazzini's package. Or maybe she'd left it deliberately—he'd seen the look on her face when he
told her who it was from. Until that moment it
hadn't occurred to him that she might have thought
that he'd bought it.

It had seemed as if there'd been something on the
tip of her tongue, something she was holding back
from saying. He knew what it was about. It was
clear that Chloe wanted him to show more paternal
interest in Emma.

Well, he could do that—he could spend time with
them and satisfy Chloe that he was making an effort
with the baby. He had made a commitment that he
fully intended to honour—to be a good parent and

to treat the child as if she were his own. But he could not make himself have feelings that didn't come naturally. Feelings that simply weren't there.

CHAPTER TEN

'I'M SO glad you're starting to get to know Emma,' Chloe said impulsively as she watched Lorenzo playing with the baby—although *playing* wasn't really the right word to describe it. And Lorenzo didn't exactly look as if he was having fun.

Nevertheless, he was patiently handing Emma a succession of soft, colourful blocks, which she took, chewed a bit, then threw back at him. She was sitting on a rug surrounded by a circle of cushions because she wasn't very stable, and Lorenzo and Chloe were sitting facing her.

Next to the baby Lorenzo seemed huge and awkward, and Chloe found herself frowning slightly as she looked at them. It was true that he was a large, powerful man, but despite his sheer size she had never seen him move or hold himself with anything but cat-like poise. Except for when he was with Emma.

'Yes.' Lorenzo's one-word response revealed just

how ill-at-ease he was feeling and Chloe found herself experiencing a hint of frustration.

She didn't know what was behind Lorenzo's lack of ease. Was he just finding the whole thing tedious? Or was he totally out of his comfort zone?

Emma was only six months old, and obviously not scintillating intellectual company. But she was fascinating and rewarding to spend time with, if you took a moment to adjust to the change of pace.

Yet Lorenzo's face was set in stone and he was not attempting to talk to her at all. Chloe wished she knew if that was just because he wasn't really interested in communicating with her, or if he felt self-conscious and unsure of what to say.

'She likes those stacking cups—the ones that are behind her,' Chloe said, wishing she could think of some way to lighten the atmosphere, but Lorenzo's oppressive silence was making her feel unsettled too.

Lorenzo didn't reply but he leant over to pick up the cups, with Emma following his movements with her bright little eyes. As he reached past her she turned her head too far and suddenly lost her balance. She rolled over sideways and knocked her head on the stack of plastic cups, and sent up a wail that echoed sharply around the room.

'Whoa!' Lorenzo said, picking her up and trying to sit her back on her bottom, but she was wailing and arching her back, and it was clear that she would just fall over again if he let go of her.

Chloe's fingers twitched with the urge to sweep the baby up, putting both her and Lorenzo out of their misery. But at the same time she didn't want to barge in. If she always did everything it would only make things harder for Lorenzo.

He really did seem to be making an effort finally. And she'd heard the concern in his voice when Emma went over. She was unbelievably glad that he did seem to be connecting with the baby on some level—even if it was only at the most basic, simple concern over her safety.

'Here, you take her,' he said suddenly, dumping the crying baby into Chloe's arms.

'Don't worry,' Chloe said, jiggling Emma to comfort her. She couldn't help feeling disappointed that he had given up so easily. But at least he had tried, she told herself. That had to be something.

'Worry?' Lorenzo said curtly. 'Worry about what?'

'That you're not finding it easy,' Chloe said. 'That you don't know what to do right away. It will come—the important thing is that you are starting to connect with her. To feel like her father.'

'No. I'm not.'

Lorenzo's bald statement of denial sent a cold chill through Chloe, and she felt an automatic need to dispute it. Of course he was starting to feel like Emma's father—he had to be.

'I'm sure that you are,' she said gently. 'Maybe

only a little. But the connection between you will grow over time.'

'I want her to be well and happy—I have made a commitment, and I fully intend to keep my word,' he said stiffly, 'but my positive intentions for the child are driven by what is the correct thing to do for her continued well-being. Not by my emotions. Not by feelings I do not have.'

Chloe stared at him, momentarily stunned by the enormity of his statement. But she could sense the frustration bubbling beneath his stern exterior—see that he was keeping something battened down inside him.

'It's understandable,' she said, treading carefully. 'She's not your flesh and blood, and she did come into your life suddenly and unexpectedly. As she gets older things will change.'

She paused, hoping for some acceptance from him. Giving him a moment to say something—anything. But he maintained an oppressive silence—a silence that Chloe felt compelled to fill. She couldn't leave things like this. She just couldn't.

'It will be different when you have your own children,' she said. 'You'll have nine months to get used to the idea of a baby. And the first time you lay eyes on it, you will love it immediately.'

'No,' Lorenzo bit out. 'There is no reason to assume I will love my children. I have told you I will do everything in my power to ensure they *feel* loved—that is the only guarantee I can make. And that is the most important thing.'

'How can you say that?' Chloe gasped. 'Of course you will love your own children. It's a natural instinct.'

'Not for everyone,' he said. 'You and I both know that to our cost. My parents did not love me—my mother sold me when I was five years old to my father as part of her divorce settlement!'

'But…but surely…at least that means your father loved you,' Chloe stumbled, horrified by Lorenzo's outburst. 'You know *he* wanted you.'

'I was nothing more than another commodity to him,' Lorenzo said bitterly.

'No.' Chloe shook her head in denial.

'Don't tell me what my childhood was like,' Lorenzo said. 'And before you start talking about natural parental instincts, perhaps you should remember how your father walked out on your seventh birthday. And your mother—she may have waited till you were grown up, but when was the last time you spoke to her?'

'Why are you being like this?' Chloe cried. 'Why would you say such horrible things?'

'To stop your unrealistic, idealised expectations,' Lorenzo grated. 'I have given you my assurance that I will be a good father—but I can't promise to feel something that is not under my control.'

'If you don't expect to love your children—why

do you even want them?' Chloe cried, jumping to her feet with Emma still in her arms and backing away from him. 'What kind of monster are you?'

Suddenly she didn't want to hear his answer—she couldn't stand to be near him a moment longer. Clutching Emma tightly, she stumbled out of the room, needing to get as far away from him as possible.

Lorenzo made no attempt to stop her leaving.

His heart was thudding violently in his chest and his palms were damp with sweat.

She had called him a monster—and maybe she was right. But all he could think about was the five-year-old boy he had once been, confused and hurting—and simply wanting his mother's warm and reassuring presence.

He didn't know anything about love. He'd never been on the receiving end of it, and he'd never felt it himself for another human being. He didn't even know if he was capable of it.

Chloe stood on the balcony that led off from the bedroom she shared with Lorenzo. It was high up on a corner of the *palazzo,* and she had a clear view out through the mouth of the Grand Canal and across the Venetian Lagoon. It was an overcast day in June, and the calm water was a muted grey, reflecting the dull, colourless sky.

Out of nowhere she found herself remembering

Lorenzo telling her about the lagoon, how the tranquil surface hid a treacherous underwater terrain of hidden channels and shifting mudflats that had protected the city against attack for centuries.

She couldn't help thinking about how that applied to Lorenzo, and how she had only just started to discover what lay beneath the surface. She'd been standing there looking out at the water for ages, while Emma took her nap, hoping the soft sea breeze would clear her head. But all she could think about was her terrible argument with him.

At first the discovery that he did not think he was capable of love had shocked and angered her. But then the more she thought about it, the more she had found herself feeling drained and heartsick. How could he have simply given up on love?

On their wedding day in February, when she'd found out that he thought marriages based on love were doomed to failure, she had been upset by how cynical he had been. But finding out that he didn't even believe that he would be able to love his own children had painted an entirely different picture.

It wasn't cynicism. It was a total lack of hope.

His life must have been so cold and empty when he was a child, but Chloe realised she knew very little about his childhood years. He had told her so much about the wonderful city he had grown up in that she'd never noticed he talked very little about himself.

Her heart ached when she thought about it. She

couldn't bear to think of him as a little boy, wandering around this *palazzo*—this huge, architectural monument to his family's great history—feeling lost and alone. And unloved.

'If you want out of this marriage, I'll understand.' Lorenzo's deep voice right behind her made her catch her breath.

'What? No…'

She spun round to face him, and was startled to see a terrible haunted look in his eyes. But then she replayed what he had just said—*if she wanted out of this marriage…*

'You made your feelings about me crystal-clear,' Lorenzo said. 'I understand if you don't want me to be the father of your children.'

'No, I…' Chloe's voice petered out as she remembered what she'd called him. 'I don't think you are a monster,' she said. 'I didn't really mean that—I've seen your good intentions towards Emma. And I know you'd only want what's best for your own children.'

'That's why I married *you,*' Lorenzo said. 'I thought *you* were best for them. I know you love Emma as if she were your own, and that you'd love all your children just as fiercely.'

He turned away for a moment, raking his hands through his short black hair in a gesture that revealed how difficult he was finding it to talk to her. Then he turned back and looked into her eyes with his troubled gaze.

'But I know that's not enough,' he said. 'Children deserve a father who is able to love them.'

Chloe looked at him, filled with a mixture of shock and despair.

She loved Lorenzo and had committed herself to making their marriage work, despite his lack of confidence in love. But now, out of the blue, he had decided not to bother.

'Are you telling me you're not man enough to stick with this?' She did not hide the disgust from her voice. 'You're the one who pushed me into this, who told me it was for the best. And now, just like that, you're prepared to give up?'

'I'm not giving up,' Lorenzo grated, clearly angered by her words. 'I've made a considered decision. This marriage was never what you wanted—not once you knew my true feelings. Why would you fight for it now?'

'Because I don't give up that easily!' Chloe cried. 'I don't turn my back on something the moment the going gets tough.'

She pushed past him into the bedroom, intending to take Emma and go for a walk to cool off. But then she remembered what she had been thinking about when Lorenzo first came in. That his troubled, *unloved* childhood had made him lose faith in people. Had made him relinquish hope for love. Maybe that was driving his decision to give up on their marriage.

She turned back to him again, the anger that had been pulsing round her body suddenly going quiet. He had been badly hurt. Maybe he was scared that he would hurt his own children.

'I don't give up that easily,' Chloe repeated, but this time more gently. 'I know your mother's desertion hurt you and that you grew up feeling unloved. But history doesn't have to repeat itself. You have to give yourself a chance.'

She stared up into his blue eyes, which were as overcast and grey-tinged as the sky above them. She wanted to find a way to reach out to him—to help him deal with the fallout of his troubled childhood.

She took a tentative step closer and lifted her hand to touch his cheek.

His reaction was instant. It was as if steel shutters dropped down over the tiny window into his soul that she'd momentarily glimpsed, and he brushed her hand aside abruptly. His rejection of her attempt to make a connection with him was total.

'Don't touch me!' he bit out. 'I don't want your sympathy. And I don't want to hear your amateur psychoanalysis of my life. Pack your bags—we're leaving for England tonight.'

He stormed out of the bedroom, leaving Chloe staring after him in a state of shock.

Had he just told her that he was divorcing her? That he was taking her back to England because their marriage was over?

CHAPTER ELEVEN

THE flight from Venice back to southern England was not long, but it turned out to be one of the most stressful flights Chloe could remember.

Emma, who had so far been very good on aeroplanes, started crying the minute they took off. By the time they were flying over the Alps, she was howling at the top of her lungs.

'What's wrong with her?' Lorenzo demanded loudly, staring at her with a horrified scowl on his face. 'Why is she doing that? She's always been all right before.'

'I don't know,' Chloe said in exasperation—she'd already tried everything she could think of to calm Emma down. There'd been an oppressive tension between Lorenzo and herself since their argument, but his agitation over Emma's crying was making things even more strained between them. 'I've never seen her like this.'

'Maybe it's her ears,' Lorenzo suddenly suggested. 'We're very high over the mountains—perhaps her ears are sensitive to the change of pressure.'

'It could be that.' Chloe seized on the idea hopefully. She was desperate to find a reason for the poor little thing's distress, and anxious to find a way to make her feel better. 'Could you pass me her drink, please? Maybe that will help.'

Sure enough, sucking on her drink did seem to calm Emma a little, and Chloe looked over at Lorenzo with relief.

'Maybe a doctor should examine her when we arrive,' Lorenzo suggested. 'She doesn't look quite right to me.'

'Maybe, although I don't think she has a fever.' Chloe frowned and tried to look down at Emma, but it was hard to see her properly because of the way she was positioned on her lap. She didn't want to move her and risk setting her off again. 'She's never been so upset before—but it doesn't necessarily mean it's something serious.'

She drew her lip into her mouth in consternation. She wanted to do whatever was best for Emma—only she didn't know whether she was just over-tired from travelling and needed a settled night at home. Or if there was really something wrong.

However, by the time they'd nearly reached the glass-walled house, the decision was made for them. After falling asleep for a short while on leaving the airport, Emma had woken up fretful and hot. Then she'd starting screaming louder than anything Chloe had ever heard before.

'We're taking her to the hospital in the next town,' Lorenzo said, barking instructions to the limousine driver to change route. 'They have a children's accident and emergency unit there—it will be the quickest way to get her seen.'

Chloe tried to sooth Emma anxiously, thankful that it didn't take long to reach the hospital.

Then all of a sudden the high-pitched crying stopped, and the baby seemed to calm down. But Chloe knew it wasn't right. From screaming so energetically, Emma had quickly become listless and dopey.

'Something's wrong,' she said, startled by how loud her voice sounded in the sudden silence in the limousine. 'We'd better find a doctor.'

'This way.' Lorenzo helped Chloe out of the vehicle, and quickly scanned the hospital signs to establish where to go.

His heart had started to thud loudly in his chest, and a crushing sensation of helplessness suddenly seized him.

Emma was so tiny. It was his responsibility to take care of her—to make sure she was all right. But he did not know what to do to make her better. The only thing he could do was to take her as quickly as possible to someone who was qualified.

Her little head was resting on Chloe's shoulder,

but it was rocking from side to side as Chloe walked, as if she did not have the strength to support it. He wanted to reach out and steady her, but he knew Emma was never truly comfortable whenever he tried to hold her. If he touched her, even just to support her head, it would probably just upset her again.

Frustration coiled through him, mixed with anger at his own inadequacy.

Why was he so incapable of taking care of an infant? He wanted to be able to do it—but no matter how hard he tried he always messed it up.

Suddenly he couldn't bear it any longer. He reached out and drew Chloe to his side, then cupped his large hand around Emma's head as they walked together.

He felt something warm and wet on his fingers.

'What's that?' he demanded, stopping in his tracks and studying Emma. 'It's coming from her ear!'

He swore in Italian, and reached out to take her from Chloe. Fear for the baby suddenly gripped him, and he strode through the doors of the emergency unit knowing implicitly that he would gain the doctor's attention more quickly.

'I need a doctor.' His voice cut through the background buzz of the waiting room. 'My baby is not well.'

* * *

Later that night Lorenzo watched Chloe lay Emma down to sleep in her cot in the glass-walled house. She was suffering from a nasty ear infection, and, although she probably still felt poorly, her temperature was down and the acute pain she had been experiencing had passed, since her eardrum had perforated and released the pressure.

'It must have hurt so much,' Chloe said, rubbing her hand over her own ear, as if she was suffering in sympathy.

'Yes, it must have been excruciating. And I can't believe that it could happen again,' Lorenzo replied, remembering what the doctor said about some children being prone to ear infections. 'I don't think I can stand to imagine how much pain she's in if she starts crying like that again.'

'Let's hope it's a one-off thing,' Chloe said. 'The doctor said that boys have a greater tendency to ear infections than girls.'

She sat down on the edge of the bed and looked up at him. There was an interested light in her green eyes, and suddenly he realised she was watching him pace up and down the bedroom.

He was showing a degree of agitation that she had probably never seen in him before. Hell—he'd rarely seen it in himself before.

'That was unbearable,' Lorenzo said. 'But at least if it does happen again I'll know what's going on. I have never felt so helpless and scared as when I saw that ooze coming out of her ear.'

He shuddered, scrubbing his hands over his face.

'I think you are starting to feel like a parent,' Chloe said gently.

He stopped pacing and stared down at her, thinking about what she had said. Maybe she was right.

Earlier, when he'd carried Emma into the examination room with ooze seeping from her ear, his heart had thudded painfully hard in his chest, and a terrible tightness had gripped his throat, making it hurt to speak. He'd waited in a state of agony, until the doctor had said that Emma would be all right, and explained what had happened.

Lorenzo sat down on the bed next to Chloe without speaking and looked at Emma, who was now sleeping in the cot.

'I think that maybe you are starting to love her,' Chloe added quietly, reaching out and taking his hand in both of hers.

A tremor passed through Lorenzo. And he squeezed Chloe's hands with his.

Over the next few days Chloe spent all her time caring for Emma. The antibiotics seemed to do their job and the baby quickly bounced back from her ear infection, becoming her normal sunny self in next to no time.

Unfortunately Lorenzo also reverted back to his typical character—emotionally withdrawn and uncommunicative—leaving Chloe feeling confused and lost.

When they'd flown back from Venice, she'd been convinced that their marriage was at breaking point—that he was bringing her to England to divorce her and cut her and Emma out of his life. She was no longer worried about that, because Lorenzo finally seemed to have made a genuine connection with Emma.

The night they'd returned from the hospital and sat together holding hands, Chloe had also felt that they'd made real progress in their personal relationship. Lorenzo had begun to reveal the depth of his concern for Emma, and for the first time ever he had not rebuffed Chloe's suggestion that he was starting to experience parental feelings—and possibly even the beginnings of love for the baby.

Chloe had fallen asleep that night with a newfound hope warming her heart. Of course it was wonderful for Lorenzo and Emma, but she also dared to believe it would bring them all closer together as a family. And if Lorenzo could feel the beginnings of love for Emma—maybe there was a chance that he could grow to love her too.

But she had been mistaken.

As the days went by Lorenzo never mentioned the conversation that had given Chloe such hope again, and his taciturn mood meant she didn't dare to raise the subject. He did start spending extra time with Emma—but his attitude towards Chloe did not appear to change at all, apart from becoming even more reticent if that was possible.

She began to feel a shadow of despair creeping over her. It was as if as soon as Lorenzo's emotional barricades had started to break down, he had deliberately set about building them up again.

Chloe spent her time wandering around the house and garden with Emma. After a while she started to feel cooped up and claustrophobic—it was a large property, but there was nowhere else for her to go. The winding country lane had no footpath beside it, and wasn't suitable for walking along, especially with a pushchair.

She began to feel her life was on hold. Lorenzo wasn't communicating with her, and she found herself seeking Mrs Guest's comforting presence more and more.

'Emma looks so much better now,' the housekeeper said, looking across from the kitchen sink, where she was preparing vegetables.

'Yes, she does,' Chloe agreed, pausing for a moment to wipe a splodge of apple purée off the baby's cheek. She had taken to giving Emma her meals in the kitchen—it made her feel less lonely.

'A much better appetite,' Mrs Guest added.

'Yes, she's nearly finished this,' Chloe said. 'Do you know if Lorenzo has any other cars here, besides the limo and the convertible?' she added, suddenly changing the subject. 'Something a bit more ordinary?'

Mrs Guest laughed.

'I don't know,' she said. 'I can ask my husband if you'd like. Are you thinking of going out on your own with Emma, and want to drive something you're more used to?'

'It was just an idea,' Chloe replied, popping the last tiny spoonful of fruit into Emma's mouth. 'There's no need for you to ask—I can do that myself.'

'I'll clean up here,' Mrs Guest said, crossing the room to wipe over the high chair. 'Why don't you take Emma out into the garden? The forecast said rain later—so you might not have a chance if you wait.'

Chloe followed Mrs Guest's suggestion, and went outside with Emma to continue their exploration of the garden. She was so grateful that it was a vibrant time of year in nature, with long daylight hours ensuring plenty of growth and changes in the garden every day. It gave her something to concentrate her attention on—and Chloe realised it was something she had missed living in the city.

The purple irises beside the pond had faded, but the water lilies had come out in a mass of impressive cream and white flowers. And the buds she'd seen on the roses climbing over the pergola had opened into full, wonderfully scented blooms.

Mr Guest had put up bird-nesting boxes in a couple of big trees near the pond, and Chloe loved to see the acrobatic blue tit parents coming and going with a flash of blue and yellow feathers. She sat down on a bench with Emma on her lap to watch them. Mr Guest had told her he expected the young birds to fledge any day—and Chloe thought it would be amazing to catch sight of the fledglings leaving the nest box.

A few minutes later a crunch on the gravel path told her that someone was approaching. It was probably Lorenzo, because the friendly gardener usually went about his work whistling cheerfully.

Her stomach turned over with nerves, and then she looked up straight into Lorenzo's blue eyes.

'Hello,' he said, sitting down beside her and reaching for Emma. 'How is she today?' he asked, turning Emma round to face him with none of the awkwardness he'd displayed only a few days before. Then he held her standing on his knees, so she could partially take her weight with her own legs and bounce up and down, as if Lorenzo's lap was her own private trampoline.

'She's fine,' Chloe said shortly, unaccountably irritated by how natural Lorenzo now seemed with Emma.

It didn't seem fair that her stomach screwed up in knots when he approached, and yet apparently he'd completely got over his uncertain floundering with the infant.

'I have been thinking about our plan to have more children,' Lorenzo said.

'Our plan?' Chloe turned sideways on the bench and stared at him. 'I thought our plan was to wait until things are settled—until we are properly used to our new circumstances.'

Lorenzo's comment seemed to be completely out of the blue. Surely he was not about to say that he thought they should start trying for a baby. They'd only been back together for a few weeks. To Chloe it still seemed as though everything was up in the air.

'We agreed that we want children,' Lorenzo said, 'and I can't see any point in waiting. It would be better for Emma if our first biological child is as close in age to her as possible.'

'I can't believe you're serious!' Chloe gasped. 'Have you forgotten what you said to me just before we left Venice? You were ready to give up on this marriage. In fact I thought that was why you'd brought me back to England—so you could leave me here, then go and get on with your life.'

'I have not forgotten.' Lorenzo's voice was strained, as if he did not appreciate being reminded of that particular conversation. 'But things are different now.'

'No, they're not!' Chloe exclaimed. 'Just because you've had your own personal epiphany—realising you *are* capable of basic human feelings towards a baby—doesn't mean we are ready to bring more children into this marriage.'

'You are a natural mother. I thought having your own baby would give you a focus in your life. Help you move on after losing your friend,' Lorenzo said calmly, despite Chloe's rising agitation.

'Don't patronise me!' Chloe gasped. 'I've got Emma to look after. I don't need another baby to help me forget my friend.'

'I didn't mean it like that—of course I am not telling you to forget your friend. But it doesn't seem as if you have fully committed to this marriage. I thought maybe a baby—'

'No!' Chloe interrupted. 'You can't solve our problems with a baby. How can you even think of using an innocent baby like that?'

She reached across and took Emma back, then cradled her protectively in her arms.

'You knew what you were getting into when you agreed to this,' Lorenzo said harshly. 'Nothing has changed. Whatever misunderstandings we may have had in the past—*this time* you knew for certain exactly where we stood.'

'How could I have known?' Chloe cried, jumping to her feet and looking Lorenzo straight in the eye. 'I mean, really known. Until you've lived in a loveless marriage you can't know what it's like.'

'You told me to my face, the night you agreed to stay in this marriage, that you did not love me.' Lorenzo stood abruptly, towering over her once more. 'Don't start this nonsense about love again.'

'It's not nonsense!' Chloe cried.

She turned away, feeling tears stinging her eyes. She'd chosen to stay in the marriage because she loved Lorenzo, and she couldn't imagine not being with him. But she'd never guessed how hard it would be.

And now, knowing he loved Emma seemed to be making it even harder. Emma wasn't his natural child, and she'd only been in his life a few weeks, and yet he'd already opened up his heart to her. But Chloe had been in his life for more than two years. If he didn't love her by now—then she knew that he never would.

'I want this marriage to work.' Lorenzo's deep voice rumbled through her. 'But that is never going to happen if you keep throwing obstacles in the way.'

'Love is not an obstacle!' Chloe gasped, spinning round to face him once more. 'Most people would think it's essential!'

She glared up at him, and saw he was looking down at her angrily.

Suddenly she couldn't bear to talk about it any

more. There was no point. Nothing was going to change Lorenzo's point of view and the only possible outcome was further humiliation and heartache for herself.

'I need a car,' she said abruptly, changing the subject completely.

'What?' Lorenzo burst out. 'What do you need a car for?'

'The same reason anyone needs a car,' she said tersely. 'I want to be able to get around the area independently.'

'The driver will take you anywhere you want to go,' Lorenzo said.

'I said *independently*,' she replied, holding his gaze crossly.

'We already have the limo and the convertible here. I can't see any need to keep another car at this property.'

'I'm not asking for anything flashy,' Chloe said, 'just a cheap second-hand car. But if you won't get me one, I can take the convertible.'

A flash of irritation passed across Lorenzo's features.

'That is a powerful vehicle—dangerous if you're not used to driving it,' he said.

'Worried I'll drive your precious car into a ditch?' she said sarcastically. 'I do know how to drive.'

'I'm not worried you'll drive into a ditch,'

Lorenzo grated. 'I'm afraid you'll go right through the hedge—or wrap it around a tree.'

'Well, buy me a little run-around. I need to go back to the cottage before the lease runs out.'

'I'll take you—in fact we'll go together right now,' Lorenzo said.

'I want to go on my own,' Chloe replied, looking down at the baby in her arms. 'It's personal.'

'If you don't want *my* company, the driver will take you,' Lorenzo said stiffly. 'He will have instructions to wait for you outside until you are done.'

Then he turned and walked away along the gravel path.

The following morning Chloe stood at the window, watching the limousine drive away through the wrought-iron gates. Lorenzo had a business meeting in London, and Chloe assumed he intended to utilise the travelling time working on his laptop in the back of the limo.

She frowned, thinking that this was another day gone by when she couldn't go back to Liz's cottage. If she didn't go soon, she wouldn't have another chance. Gladys, Liz's kindly neighbour, would have had to return the keys to the letting agency.

Gladys had already been in and cleared the few remaining things that Chloe had left behind when Lorenzo whisked her away so suddenly. There had not been much to do—they'd already taken care of nearly everything in those heartbreakingly hollow days before the funeral.

But Chloe still had to pick up a box of letters and mementoes that Liz had packed for Emma before her illness had progressed too far.

'Let's go and get you some breakfast,' she said, scooping Emma up from where she was playing happily in her cot. 'Then we'll think of something to do today.'

But as soon as she'd spoken a plan was already forming in her mind. She would take the convertible and drive herself to the village. Lorenzo didn't need it that day—and, more importantly, he wasn't there to stop her going.

'Chloe!' Gladys exclaimed as she opened the front door of her cottage. 'What a lovely surprise. Oh, look how much Emma has grown! And you're looking well too. Come in—come in for a cup of tea, and tell me what you've been doing with yourself.'

'It's lovely to see you, too,' Chloe said, giving Gladys a hug. Then she followed her into her cheery front room, which was full of knick-knacks and drawings done by her many grandchildren.

'I'll put the kettle on,' Gladys said. 'Then you can tell me everything.'

Half an hour later Chloe gave the old lady another hug and stepped back out onto the street, carrying a sleeping Emma in her portable car seat.

'It's been lovely to see you,' Gladys said warmly. 'I wish we had longer to catch up, but I've got to pop out now. If I'm not back when you're ready to go— just put the key through the letterbox. And promise to come back and see me soon.'

'I will,' Chloe assured her. 'Thank you for the tea.'

Chloe hugged the old lady one more time and went next door to Liz's cottage, carrying Emma extra-carefully to avoid waking her up. As she opened the front door the familiar scent of Liz's essential-oil burner wafted over her, sending her straight back to the time she had lived there with her friend.

She sat down on the sofa and pulled Liz's box of memories close to her. Up until that moment she hadn't had the heart to open it. But now she realised that she should do it here—where she had shared Liz's last few months.

She lifted the lid gingerly, and right on the top was an envelope addressed to her in Liz's handwriting. Her heart constricted and her hand was shaking as she lifted the letter. It was not a long letter, and the handwriting was spidery, as if Liz had struggled to find the physical strength to write it.

Dear Chloe
You have always been my best friend, and it has meant so much to me having you with me these last few months.

You are a wonderful person, with a kind, true heart, and I wish you only the best in life.

There are no words to express what it means to me, knowing that Emma will be with you when I am gone. There is no one in the world I would rather bring up my precious daughter, and I trust you completely to do what is right for her.

But Chloe, promise me that you will not give up on your own happiness. I know you have been hurt in the past, but don't let that stop you taking a chance on love. I truly believe that it's better to regret the things that don't work out in the way you'd hoped, than regret not taking a chance on something that could be amazing.

Thank you from the bottom of my heart, for everything you have done for me, and will continue to do for me through Emma after I am gone. You have been the most loyal and wonderful friend anyone could ever ask for and I feel truly blessed to have had you in my life.

All my love, always.
Your best friend forever, Liz.

Chloe slipped the letter back into the envelope with a shaking hand. She didn't realise she was weeping until she saw a tear splash onto the envelope, making the blue ink start to run. She missed Liz so much, although she knew she'd always be in her heart. And she'd always cherish the memories of her friendship.

But Liz's words in the letter about taking a chance on love had been difficult to read. That was exactly what Chloe had done by staying with Lorenzo—but it was turning out so much more painful than Chloe could have imagined.

Lorenzo gripped the steering wheel, fury eating through him as fast as the powerful limousine ate up the miles to the village.

He could not believe that Chloe had taken the convertible. He hadn't known she had it in her to show such defiance—to deliberately disobey a direct order from him. He'd only forbidden her to drive for her own safety. The roads were narrow and winding, with sudden bends that took drivers by surprise. And the convertible was an exceptionally powerful car— a steel deathtrap in inexperienced hands.

When he found Chloe he would demand an explanation. He would let her know that it was not acceptable for her to defy him—that he would not tolerate it.

Suddenly, as he approached a tight bend, a metallic shaft of light flashed in his eye. A car had driven off the road ahead of him—the driver failing to make the sharp turn in time.

'Chloe!' Her name burst from his lips and he felt his heart crash painfully against his ribs.

He slammed on the brakes, almost losing control of the limo, and pulled off the road into an entrance to a field. He was out of his seat in a second, sprinting back to where the other car had gone through the hedge.

He clambered through the broken gap in the hedgerow, oblivious to the brambles clawing at his legs, and realised that it was not the convertible. In fact it was not even the same colour or model car. He had been thinking so hard about Chloe that his mind had played a vicious trick on him.

Filled with a mixture of relief and edginess, he hurried to the vehicle, to check if anyone needed his help. The car was abandoned. The driver and any passengers had already left the scene. He laid his hand above the engine, and confirmed that the car was cold—the accident had happened some time ago.

He walked shakily back to the limo, realising he had broken out into a cold sweat. The thought of Chloe being in an accident had terrified him. He leant against the rusty five-bar gate into the field and took some deep steadying breaths.

The only other time he could remember having felt anything like it was the night of Emma's ear infection. But this time his reaction had been even more acute. He told himself that it must be because there was a car crash involved. Car crashes were sudden and violent, and were potentially fatal.

He got back into the limo and headed onwards in the direction of the village—driving much more slowly. Then, when he reached the row of cottages and saw the convertible parked at the side of the street, he felt a second, even more intense wave of relief.

Chloe had given him a nasty fright. He would make sure she never did such a thing again.

He got out of the car angrily and walked to the cottage, glancing in through the front-room window as he approached the front door. What he saw stopped him in his tracks.

Chloe was weeping. She was sitting on the sofa, with her face buried in her hands and her whole body wracked with sobs.

A pain as sharp as a knife twisted in his stomach as he watched her.

He wanted to go in and comfort her. To wrap his arms tenderly around her and take her away from whatever was causing her such distress.

But she had not wanted him there. She had made that very clear. She had told him it was personal and that she wanted to be alone.

Suddenly, he knew that he could not disturb her. His presence would make her suffering even worse.

He turned silently away. Then he repositioned the limousine further along the street so she would not see it when she left, and sat quietly waiting for her to leave. From a distance he would check she was all right. And then he would follow her home.

CHAPTER TWELVE

CHLOE stood by the floor-to-ceiling window in the bedroom, looking out over the pre-dawn landscape. It was not much past 4:00 a.m., but the dim, colourless light of dawn was creeping across the sky.

She couldn't sleep. She was thinking of the time she'd told Lorenzo about the house of her dreams—the house which she thought had been the inspiration behind the purchase of this property they were currently living in.

It was about a year after she'd started working for him, and they had driven out of London for a business meeting with a man who'd refused to leave his home in Sussex to meet with Lorenzo in London. Chloe had loved the journey, sitting next to her gorgeous boss in the front of his sports car, chattering away about inconsequential things.

Then all of a sudden something about the countryside and the narrow, twisting roads had made her remember a house she'd visited once as a child. Her aunt had worked as a housekeeper, performing a very similar role to Mrs Guest, and one summer, when the owners of the house were away travelling, she had invited Chloe, her sister and mother to visit.

Chloe had been absolutely entranced by the place. She had never seen whole walls made out of glass before—except in high-street shops—and she'd thought they were magical. Her sister had been scared of heights, and wouldn't go near the upstairs windows. But Chloe had leant spreadeagled against the glass and it felt as if she were flying over the fields.

Her mum and aunt had shooed her away, worrying about fingerprints on the window, and then Chloe had heard them talking, saying who'd want such a ridiculous amount of glass to keep clean? But Chloe hadn't cared about that—she'd simply loved the feeling of flying, and had made a wish that one day she would live in a house like that.

It was amazing that Lorenzo had remembered. And that he had taken the trouble to find this house for her as a wedding gift.

Right from the start of their relationship he had always been attentive and thoughtful. It was all those gestures that had made her believe that he loved her, even though he had never told her.

Now she didn't know what to think. How was it possible for him to pay so much attention to little things that he knew would make her happy—yet continually throw her love back in her face? Why did he act as if she were committing some terrible moral crime, simply by having feelings for him?

Chloe ran her fingers through her hair, brushing it back off her face, and sighed. A pale hint of apricot tinged the eastern sky, and she realised the sunrise was coming. The giant window would give her an amazing view.

Suddenly it occurred to her that the birds should be singing. The dawn chorus would be underway by now, but she couldn't hear a thing. The triple-glazed, reinforced glass cut out the sounds of the outside world as effectively as a sound-proofed room.

The thought upset her. At that moment it seemed like a terrible reflection of her marriage with Lorenzo. She had a perfect view—but she wasn't really living it. All the birds out there were triumphantly singing to welcome in the dawn—but she couldn't even hear the tiniest peep.

Without thinking what she was doing, she walked silently across the room to pick up her dressing gown, then went downstairs to let herself out into the garden.

But she couldn't get out. The kitchen door was locked and she couldn't remember where the key was kept.

She hurried through to the living room, to try the French windows, but when she got there she realised she had no idea how to open them. She knew they were motorised and she thought there was a remote control somewhere, or a panel on the wall, but she couldn't find anything.

Tears started to flow down her face as she stared helplessly out through the massive glass doors.

Lorenzo lay awake in bed, aware that Chloe was not beside him. He knew she hadn't been sleeping well and often rose before dawn, to stand looking out at the view over the countryside. But now he couldn't remember the last time he'd heard her moving around.

Suddenly he realised the room was extra-still. He could hear Emma snuffling in her sleep through the open door into the adjacent room. But he could not hear Chloe.

He sat up, and instantly saw she had gone.

His heart thudded and he lurched out of bed. She'd run away—walked out on their marriage again.

Then he forced himself to stay calm. He knew she would never leave Emma. She'd probably gone down to the kitchen to make herself a drink. He'd seen the half-drunk cups of chamomile tea beside her bed in the morning, and known they hadn't been there when he went to bed at night.

But that morning he sensed something was different. She'd been so upset the previous day. What if she had realised she couldn't stay in this marriage? What if she was planning to leave him?

The thought sent dread crashing through his veins

once again. He pulled on his trousers and was out of the room, running down the staircase immediately.

Then he saw her. She was at the French windows, trying to find the way to open them.

'What are you doing?' he barked, his fear making his voice hard. 'Where are you going at four-thirty in the morning?'

'Nowhere.' She turned to face him and he saw that she was weeping.

A vicious spear of agony stabbed through him. She was distraught once more—and he knew it was his fault. He was incapable of making her happy, and that knowledge was killing him.

'I'm sorry,' he said, pulling her gently into his arms. He knew it wouldn't make her feel better— how could it when she was so unhappy being with him? But he didn't know what else to do.

'I couldn't open the doors.' Her voice was muffled against his chest, but Lorenzo could hear the notes of agony in it.

'If you want to leave, I won't stop you—you deserve to be happy,' he said. 'But don't run away from me again. Let me help you. Let me make sure you are all right.'

Chloe pulled away and looked up at him. His words had startled her. It sounded as if he cared about her. But at the same time it sounded as if he was offering to help her escape from their marriage.

'I wasn't leaving,' she said, wiping the palm of

her hand across her face. 'I wanted to go outside to hear the birds singing—the dawn chorus.'

'Thank God!' Lorenzo exclaimed, crushing her against him. 'I couldn't stand it—I just couldn't stand my life without you.'

Chloe drew in a shaky breath, having difficulty breathing—both from Lorenzo's lung-crushing grip and from the words he had said. Did it mean he truly wanted her in his life? That he did have feelings for her?

'No matter what—I'll never leave you.' Her voice was squeaky with breathlessness, but then he relaxed his grip slightly to look down at her.

'But you are so unhappy with me,' Lorenzo said, confusion showing on his face and in his voice.

'I'll never leave you, because I love you,' she said simply. 'I've always loved you, and it breaks my heart that you can't love me back. But I can't even imagine not being with you any more.'

A change came over Lorenzo's expression. His eyes hardened and a muscle started throbbing in his jaw. He shook his head slightly, and even shrank back a little, as if he totally denied what she had told him.

A rush of despair rose up in Chloe. It was just like the first time she had opened her heart to him on their wedding day.

'Why don't you believe me?' she cried. 'What have I ever done to make you have no trust in what I say?'

She lifted her hand to her head, suddenly feeling dizzy from lack of sleep and stress, but she stared up into Lorenzo's face. The expression of rejection she saw there cut her to the quick.

'Why can't you look into my eyes, and see that it's true?' she demanded. 'I love you so much it hurts. But all you do is look at me like that—like I'm lying.'

Lorenzo stared down at Chloe, her distraught expression making it feel as if there were a blade twisting in his guts.

Overwhelming emotion surged through his body, and he didn't know how to handle it. He looked down into her tortured face and saw how overwrought she was. *He* had done that. *He* was the reason she was so distressed.

'I'm sorry,' he said. 'I've messed everything up so badly. I don't know how I can ever put it right.'

'It's not your fault,' she said, sounding utterly dejected. 'It's not your fault you don't feel the same as I do. You can't make yourself fall in love with someone.'

There was a terrible look of despair on her face, which intensified when Lorenzo didn't say anything. But he didn't know *how* to respond.

He had never meant to hurt Chloe, yet he had found himself doing it again and again. Why hadn't it been possible for him to find some response—any response—that would not have torn her heart apart?

Why wasn't he able to feel what she wanted him to feel?

'All I want is your happiness,' he said, reaching out to pull her into his arms. 'I don't know why it's so difficult for me to make that happen. I know I'm breaking your heart—and it's breaking my heart too.'

Chloe closed her eyes and leant against his strong body, feeling a rush of emotion rising through her as she took in Lorenzo's anguish. She had never heard him express such strong feelings before—surely it had to mean something? That perhaps he wasn't the cold, emotionally unavailable man he claimed to be?

'I'm sorry,' he gasped, letting go and holding her away from him. 'I'm suffocating you.'

'It's all right,' she wheezed. 'I like being in your arms—it feels right.'

'Yes, it does!' he exploded, raking his hands violently through his short black hair. 'It feels so right—it has always felt right. So why do I keep hurting you so badly?'

He cursed again, and Chloe could see his hands were shaking.

'You need to get away from me—so that I can't bring you any more pain.' He took a step backwards, looking down at her with wild, anguished eyes.

She stared up at him—startled by his outburst and shaken by the intensity of it, but at the same time mesmerised by his words. Had he really begun to express something she had almost stopped hoping for—something of unbelievable wonder?

'I'm sorry,' he said. 'You deserve so much more than this—you deserve to be loved. You were right about why I brought you back here. I tried to do the right thing—to let you go before I brought you any more heartache. But I just wasn't strong enough to do it. Even though I kept hurting you—I couldn't bring myself to leave you.'

'I don't want you to leave me,' Chloe said, tears sparkling in her eyes. But she held herself in check—she didn't want to do anything to send Lorenzo off the wonderful road of understanding that she hoped and prayed he was finally travelling. 'I never want you to leave me.'

'But why?' Lorenzo demanded, an agonised expression contorting his face. 'Despite my attempts to make you happy—all I've ever done is bring you misery!'

'You *know* why I don't ever want to leave you.' Chloe stepped forward and laid her hand gently on his cheek, and suddenly Lorenzo stilled—as if the fury and rage evaporated.

'I don't…I can't believe…' he stumbled, his blue eyes confused and troubled as he looked deep into hers.

'Then tell me why you have tried to make me happy,' Chloe said. She lifted her other hand and held his face, trying to give him the strength and confidence to accept what she believed to be unfolding in his heart.

'Because…' Lorenzo stared down at her with wide, glistening eyes. His emotion was so raw, so overwhelming to him that her soul ached for him.

Chloe moved her hands gently, smoothing the moisture from his cheeks. But she looked steadily into his eyes, as if she were holding his heart with her gaze.

'Because…I love you.'

Lorenzo's voice was so quiet that Chloe could barely hear him. But the heartfelt expression in his eyes told her what she had yearned to hear for so long. Her own eyes burned with joy and suddenly the tears started to fall. Her heart was overflowing with love for Lorenzo, and finally she knew that he felt the same way.

'Are they tears of happiness?' Lorenzo said gruffly, almost hesitantly, as he stared down into the face of the woman he loved—*the woman he loved*.

'Yes.' Chloe nodded, wiping her hands over her face and gazing up at him with luminous green eyes. 'Of course they are.'

A smile broke out over Lorenzo's face and he felt his heart swell to bursting.

He was in love.

In love with Chloe.

He gazed down at her, filled with the most amazing sensation of awe. How was it possible for him to feel this way?

She looked like an angel. Heavenly beauty glowed from deep within her, and Lorenzo knew he was looking at the face of love.

'I don't deserve this,' he murmured, sliding his fingers into her blonde hair and cradling her head.

'Why not?' she asked. 'Everyone deserves to love and feel loved.'

'But…it's not…' he stumbled. 'My mother…'

'The fact that your mother was a heartless witch does not mean you are like her—or that you don't have the capacity for love,' Chloe said, suddenly sounding angrier than Lorenzo had ever heard her. 'That woman trampled your heart and bound you up inside. What she did was unforgivable—but you can't let it affect your whole life.'

Lorenzo stared down at her in shock. But her impassioned outburst had struck a chord deep inside him. She knew him so well.

Another rush of emotion stormed up through him, overwhelming him once again. He cleared his throat gruffly, and stepped away to look out of the window.

'No, don't turn away from me,' Chloe said, pulling him back towards her. 'I love you—and I won't let you shut me out again.'

Lorenzo felt himself smiling.

A bubble of laughter burst out of him. He was in love with Chloe and she was taking no prisoners.

'You've been battening down your heart for too long,' she said, thumping him playfully on the chest. 'But now we've broken it free—don't think I'm going to let you get away with closing it up again.'

He caught her hands in his, and gathered them up to him, looking seriously into her eyes once more.

'I've been a fool,' he said, with heart-wrenching honesty. 'I put so much energy into convincing myself that love was a lie—that it didn't really exist. I thought I'd found another way to build my life, a practical approach that wouldn't let me down. When you said you loved me I was angry. In one fell swoop you undermined everything I had set up to be true. I think even then I knew you were telling me the truth, but I couldn't let myself believe it.'

'You believe it now,' Chloe said. 'That's the most important thing.'

'But we wasted so much time,' he said, shaking his head as he thought about the months they'd spent apart.

'It wasn't wasted,' she said earnestly. 'Not if that was what was necessary to reach through to your heart.'

Lorenzo looked down at her, feeling another wave of emotion rising through him. She was amazing.

'You are the best part of me,' he said, reaching out to her again and drawing her into his arms. 'Without you I was nothing. Don't ever leave me.'

Chloe closed her eyes and gave herself over to the awe-inspiring depth of emotion that was flowing through her body. She'd always loved him—but this was something different. Somehow knowing that her love was reciprocated had magnified the wonder of it a hundredfold.

She had never been so happy, and she had never been filled with so much hope for the future. She leant into his embrace, knowing that she had finally found what her heart had been searching for.

A few wonderful moments later, she felt herself being lifted into his arms, and he carried her back up to their bedroom. As they passed through the doorway the sound of Emma chatting to herself in her cot drifted through to her consciousness.

'I'll get her,' Lorenzo said, placing a lingering kiss on her lips before walking through the open door into Emma's nursery next to their bedroom.

Chloe watched with happiness as he carried her in. He looked so comfortable with the baby girl. He had made a true connection with her and Chloe knew truly he was ready to be her father emotionally as well as practically.

'Let's sit here a while,' he said, getting onto the bed and placing Emma on the soft cover.

Chloe smiled and picked up a handful of toys before joining them.

'You know, she can't balance very well on here,' she said, crawling into the centre of the king-sized bed to sit with them. 'It's too wobbly.'

'I'll hold her,' Lorenzo said, sitting her between his legs and gently supporting her little body. 'I just want to sit here for a while, with my family close to me.'

Chloe felt her eyes tingle with tears once again. She looked at him holding Emma and she suddenly knew she had never seen a more beautiful sight. He looked completely relaxed, sitting with his little baby daughter.

He lifted his glowing eyes and caught her gaze with his.

'Come closer,' he said, holding out his arm. 'I want both my girls close to me.'

Chloe smiled and moved across the bed, careful not to wobble Emma off balance, although she knew Lorenzo had her.

She snuggled up against him, revelling in the warm strength of his arm around her. It felt truly wonderful sitting there. Then suddenly she heard the familiar rustle of a foil packet coming from his trouser pocket as he shifted his position slightly.

At that moment she made another decision—or rather she knew that the time was right to take the next step.

She slipped her hand into his pocket and drew out the condom packet.

'Hmm.' Lorenzo made an approving sound. 'But I think it's still a bit too early to take Emma down to Mrs Guest.'

'That's OK,' Chloe said. 'We'll be alone later. But we won't be needing this.'

With that she tossed the little packet away, towards the waste-paper basket under the dressing table.

She felt a tremble pass through Lorenzo, and she looked up to see the shimmer of moisture in his eyes once more.

'I love you,' he said.

The following morning, before the cool light of dawn started to creep over the horizon, Chloe felt Lorenzo lifting her gently out of bed.

'Come with me,' he murmured in her ear, drawing her out of a deep, restful sleep. 'I have a surprise for you.'

'What is it?' Chloe asked dreamily. Her body was still fabulously relaxed, and glowing from the aftermath of the most wonderful lovemaking they had ever shared. Somehow, knowing that a new life might form inside her because of it had made it even more magical than usual. 'It's the middle of the night—where are you taking me?'

'It's not the middle of the night,' Lorenzo said, carrying her out of the bedroom, duvet and all.

He took her downstairs, then pressed a button on the concealed control panel, and the giant sliding doors in the living room glided open.

Chloe drew in a surprised breath of fresh pre-dawn air, but her body was still cosy, wrapped up snugly in the duvet.

'I've got us a front row seat,' Lorenzo said, carrying her across the glistening dew-covered lawn towards the bench that overlooked the meadow. 'With full surround sound.'

Chloe smiled—completely speechless. She couldn't believe he had planned this, woken up hours before he had to, just to bring her outside for the dawn chorus.

They sat together on the bench, watching the golden tinge in the east unfold into the most beautiful sunrise Chloe had ever seen, and listening to the sound of myriad birds greeting the new day in a truly magnificent ensemble.

'Thank you,' Chloe breathed when the symphony of birdsong had eased from its glorious crescendo. 'That was the most amazing thing anyone has ever done for me.'

'You're welcome,' Lorenzo said. 'All I want, more than anything in the world, is to make you happy.'

'All I need to make me happy is your love,' she replied, gazing up into the face of the man she adored.

'Chloe Valente, I love you,' he said, his voice vibrating with powerful, heartfelt emotion. 'I love you more than I can say. And I always will.'

* * * * *

Harlequin Intrigue top author Delores Fossen presents a brand-new series of breathtaking romantic suspense!
TEXAS MATERNITY: HOSTAGES
The first installment available May 2010:
THE BABY'S GUARDIAN

Shaw cursed and hooked his arm around Sabrina.

Despite the urgency that the deadly gunfire created, he tried to be careful with her, and he took the brunt of the fall when he pulled her to the ground. His shoulder hit hard, but he held on tight to his gun so that it wouldn't be jarred from his hand.

Shaw didn't stop there. He crawled over Sabrina, sheltering her pregnant belly with his body, and he came up ready to return fire.

This was obviously a situation he'd wanted to avoid at all cost. He didn't want his baby in the middle of a fight with these armed fugitives, but when they fired that shot, they'd left him no choice. Now, the trick was to get Sabrina safely out of there.

"Get down," someone on the SWAT team yelled from the roof of the adjacent building.

Shaw did. He dropped lower, covering Sabrina as best he could.

There was another shot, but this one came from a rifleman on the SWAT team. Shaw didn't look up, but he heard the sound of glass being blown apart.

The shots continued, all coming from his men, which meant it might be time to try to get Sabrina to better cover. Shaw glanced at the front of the building.

So that Sabrina's pregnant belly wouldn't be smashed against the ground, Shaw eased off her and moved her to a sitting position so that her back was against the brick wall. They were close. Too close. And face-to-face.

He found himself staring right into those sea-green eyes.

How will Shaw get Sabrina out?
Follow the daring rescue and the heartbreaking
aftermath in THE BABY'S GUARDIAN
by Delores Fossen,
available May 2010 from Harlequin Intrigue.

Bestselling Harlequin Presents® author

Lynne Graham

introduces

VIRGIN ON HER WEDDING NIGHT

Valente Lorenzatto never forgave Caroline Hales's
abandonment of him at the altar. But now he's
made millions and claimed his aristocratic Venetian
birthright—and he's poised to get his revenge.
He'll ruin Caroline's family by buying out their
company and throwing them out of their mansion...
unless she agrees to give him the wedding night
she denied him five years ago....

**Available May 2010
from Harlequin Presents!**

HARLEQUIN *Presents*

Coming Next Month

in **Harlequin Presents® EXTRA.** Available April 13, 2010.

#97 RICH, RUTHLESS AND SECRETLY ROYAL
Robyn Donald
Regally Wed

#98 FORGOTTEN MISTRESS, SECRET LOVE-CHILD
Annie West
Regally Wed

#99 TAKEN BY THE PIRATE TYCOON
Daphne Clair
Ruthless Tycoons

#100 ITALIAN MARRIAGE: IN NAME ONLY
Kathryn Ross
Ruthless Tycoons

Coming Next Month

in **Harlequin Presents®.** Available April 27, 2010:

#2915 VIRGIN ON HER WEDDING NIGHT
Lynne Graham

#2916 TAMED: THE BARBARIAN KING
Jennie Lucas
Dark-Hearted Desert Men

#2917 BLACKWOLF'S REDEMPTION
Sandra Marton
Men Without Mercy

#2918 THE PRINCE'S CHAMBERMAID
Sharon Kendrick
At His Service

#2919 MISTRESS: PREGNANT BY THE SPANISH BILLIONAIRE
Kim Lawrence

#2920 RUTHLESS RUSSIAN, LOST INNOCENCE
Chantelle Shaw

HARLEQUIN®

INTRIGUE®

REQUEST YOUR FREE BOOKS!

HARLEQUIN® *Presents*~®

PASSION GUARANTEED SEDUCTION

2 FREE NOVELS PLUS
2 FREE GIFTS!

YES! Please send me 2 FREE Harlequin Presents® novels and my 2 FREE gifts (gifts are worth about $10). After receiving them, if I don't wish to receive any more books, I can return the shipping statement marked "cancel." If I don't cancel, I will receive 6 brand-new novels every month and be billed just $4.05 per book in the U.S. or $4.74 per book in Canada. That's a saving of close to 15% off the cover price! It's quite a bargain! Shipping and handling is just 50¢ per book in the U.S. and 75¢ per book in Canada.* I understand that accepting the 2 free books and gifts places me under no obligation to buy anything. I can always return a shipment and cancel at any time. Even if I never buy another book, the two free books and gifts are mine to keep forever.

106 HDN E4FN 306 HDN E4FY

Name _____ (PLEASE PRINT) _____

Address _____ Apt. # _____

City _____ State/Prov. _____ Zip/Postal Code _____

Signature (if under 18, a parent or guardian must sign)

Mail to the **Harlequin Reader Service:**
IN U.S.A.: P.O. Box 1867, Buffalo, NY 14240-1867
IN CANADA: P.O. Box 609, Fort Erie, Ontario L2A 5X3

Not valid for current subscribers to Harlequin Presents books.

Are you a current subscriber to Harlequin Presents books and want to receive the larger-print edition? Call 1-800-873-8635 today!

* Terms and prices subject to change without notice. Prices do not include applicable taxes. N.Y. residents add applicable sales tax. Canadian residents will be charged applicable provincial taxes and GST. Offer not valid in Quebec. This offer is limited to one order per household. All orders subject to approval. Credit or debit balances in a customer's account(s) may be offset by any other outstanding balance owed by or to the customer. Please allow 4 to 6 weeks for delivery. Offer available while quantities last.

Your Privacy: Harlequin Books is committed to protecting your privacy. Our Privacy Policy is available online at www.eHarlequin.com or upon request from the Reader Service. From time to time we make our lists of customers available to reputable third parties who may have a product or service of interest to you. If you would prefer we not share your name and address, please check here. ☐

Help us get it right—We strive for accurate, respectful and relevant communications. To clarify or modify your communication preferences, visit us at www.ReaderService.com/consumerschoice.

HP10

HARLEQUIN® *Blaze*™

is proud to introduce...

New York Times bestselling author

Brenda Jackson

with

SPONTANEOUS

Kim Cannon and Duan Jeffries have a great thing going. Whenever they meet up, the passion between them is hot, intense…spontaneous. And things really heat up when Duan agrees to accompany her to her mother's wedding. Too bad there's something he's not telling her.…

Don't miss the fireworks!

Available in May 2010
wherever Harlequin Blaze books are sold.

---

red-hot reads

www.eHarlequin.com

HB79542